BURY METR

This book must be returned on or before the last date recorded below to the Library from which it was borrowed.

AUTHOR	CLASS No.
USHER, F.	J TEENAGE

TITLE	
Tell Alice	BOOK No.
	S.93

Tell Alice

Tell Alice

Frances Usher

Methuen Children's Books

For Lena

First published in Great Britain 1993
by Methuen Children's Books
an imprint of Reed Consumer Books Limited
Michelin House, 81 Fulham Road, London SW3 6RB
and Auckland, Melbourne, Singapore and Toronto

Copyright © 1993 Frances Usher

The right of Frances Usher to be identified as
author of this work has been asserted by her in
accordance with the Copyright, Designs and
Patent Act 1988

ISBN 0 416 18781 1

A CIP catalogue record for this title is
available at the British Library

Printed in Great Britain
by Bookcraft (Bath) Limited

Contents

Chapter One

'Violet what?'

'Violet Bottom,' the estate agent said again.

'The Adventures of Violet Bottom,' said Hilary Milford. 'Straight out of a comic strip. Or it might be one of those apes – a baboon, is it? Or a gibbon?'

'Oh, Mum, don't,' said Joanna. 'I think it sounds great. What an address – Number Two, Violet Bottom. I bet the garden's full of violets. And primroses.' She couldn't think of any other flowers. 'And things.'

'This time of year?'

Joanna glanced out of the window; cars were splashing down the main street of Dorchester through a thin film of sleet.

'It'll soon be spring,' she said. 'By the time we move in . . .' She looked again at the smudgy photocopied picture of the semi-detached cottage, mentally filling it with colour, feeling a spurt of certainty.

'The garden,' said the estate agent, smiling at her encouragingly, 'is well stocked and mature.'

'Overgrown,' said Hilary. 'That's what that means, I fear. And it's very isolated. Just that pair of cottages in the middle of deepest Dorset. No, really, it's not for us. Sorry.' She stood up. 'Jo, we must get back to the car before a traffic warden sees it. And then keep searching. There must be something somewhere.'

'It's a question of what you can pay for a property.' The estate agent was still frowning at the computer screen. 'Look, we've lots more modern houses here if you could just increase your price a bit . . .'

'No, we can't do that,' said Joanna, feeling her mother's warning glance on her, and choosing to ignore it. 'There are only the two of us now, you see. My dad and brother are staying on in London. So money's a bit short. But we don't want anything more modern.' She turned to Hilary, willing her to agree.

'We don't, do we, Mum? Violet Bottom's exactly what we've been looking for.'

Joanna Milford was fourteen.

Jessie Bone's older sister Alice is fourteen too. But Alice is dying.

Jessie Bone sits on the doorstep of Number Two, Violet Bottom, with her friend Minna Kellaway, and tries not to think about it. Father has told her to go next door to Minna's and to stay there.

'But, Father –' she protests. 'I could sit with Alice and sing to her. She likes that.'

'You must keep away,' Father says sternly. 'Doctor Tripp will be here soon.' He lifts the white sheet soaked in carbolic that hangs over the doorway of the bedroom to keep out the germs. Somewhere behind there lies Alice, dreadfully alone and quiet in the big bed that she's always shared with Jessie. Even the cough that has racked the house for days has faded away by this Saturday morning into a frightening silence.

'Keep away, Jessie,' Father repeats. 'A sick room is no place for a seven-year-old.' He feels her forehead. 'This terrible influenza . . .'

'I'm eight,' she's going to say, but Father has already gone back behind the sheet.

'Father,' Jessie calls. 'Tell Alice –'

Tell her what? Tell Alice . . .

Slowly, Jessie goes down the stairs. The parlour door stands half open. She crosses the musty little room to the chest of drawers in the corner, lifts out Alice's housekeeping purse from the top drawer and stands hugging it. Every Friday evening the whole family sits round the table and Father opens his wages and hands over the housekeeping money to Alice.

Some sheet music is open on the piano, duets that she's been playing with Alice. She puts out a hand and plays a few notes. Alice has said that one day Jessie will be a famous singer.

'Jessie,' Father calls down the stairs. 'Next door. At once.'

Guiltily, she puts back the purse and goes out of the front door, across the garden to the next-door cottage.

It's sheltered on the step of Minna's house, and the hazy September sunshine is warm on the little girls' faces. It's so quiet that they can hear the cows in the field across the lane cropping the grass. The leaves on the elm trees are just starting to turn yellow.

Minna takes a comb from her pinafore pocket. 'I'll do your hair for you, Jess.'

Jessie shakes her thick brown curls over her face. 'I can't get the tangles out. Alice does it usually . . .'

Through the Kellaways' open window behind them they can hear the treadle of the sewing machine, and Jessie's five-year-old brother Leonard complaining in his high little voice that he's hungry, asking Minna's mother for a biscuit.

'I don't believe I got no biscuits just at the moment, my lovey.'

Jessie can tell from Leonard's muffled protest that Mrs Kellaway is trying to hug him to her large soft chest again. 'Now you be a good boy, sweetheart, and listen out for the doctor's motor coming down the lane. Let's hope he don't get stuck in the mud. A real live motor car. You'll like that, won't you, Lenny? Poor little motherless lamb,' she adds, in a low voice.

Jessie stops herself listening.

'As soon as Alice is well again,' she says, 'she's going to teach me some new songs. I like singing with Alice.'

The comb pauses in Minna's hand. 'I'll sing with you, Jess.' Her blue eyes framed with pale lashes look anxiously at Jessie. 'I'm not as good as your Alice, mind, but we could sing together. Couldn't we?'

'Oh, yes,' Jessie says quickly. Actually, Jessie often feels her mind going scratchy when Minna sings, but she mustn't say so. Minna's her best friend and, besides, she and her mother are being so kind. Father has said they are all to be grateful for help in such hard times.

There's the flu, sweeping in from nobody knows where, making half the villagers of Lansbury Abbas nearly as sick as Alice. And there is the war, that's been going on for as long as Jessie and Minna can remember.

Minna's father is lying wounded in hospital at this very moment in a place called the Western Front. Minna has shown them all at school a postcard that he's sent home; *I am wounded and am going on well* is printed on the card, and there's a shaky signature at the bottom: *H.E. Kellaway*, and the date, *4/8/18*.

'My daddy'll be home soon,' Minna says confidently. 'I expect they'll send him back on one of them hospital trains. Anyhow, you know what the Rector said the other day. The war's going to be over this year. It won't go on into 1919. That's what he said.'

Sometimes, when Jessie's father has been reading his newspaper, he talks of the war going on for years and years more, going on so long that even Jessie's brothers Harold and Frank, who are only thirteen and eleven, will one day be taken into the army. Frank would love that, Jessie knows. To Frank, it would all be great fun; even more fun than going out ferreting at night in the grounds of the Big House with his friend Cyril Wragge and Cyril Wragge's older brothers. She doesn't think Harold would find it fun, but he'd go if he thought it was his duty. Harold is like that.

'Father says –' she begins.

'Hush.' Minna turns her head. 'Here it comes, Jess. Weren't the boys quick?'

A heavy, chugging sound is drawing nearer. The cows throw up their heads in alarm.

'Now your Alice will be all right.'

'Yes.'

A black motor car is bumping slowly into view along the narrow mud lane that leads to the cottages. Jessie's brothers Harold and Frank are perched high on the back seat. Father sent them running this morning the two miles to Lansbury Abbas to fetch the doctor when Alice's breathing grew so bad.

The engine stops with a sputter. In the sudden silence, Jessie goes on sitting still.

The doctor strides up the little path of Number One, carrying his black bag. The two boys hurry behind.

Minna's mother bustles across from the other cottage, holding Leonard's hand.

'Wants to see your motor, Doctor. Bless him.'

'Yes, well . . .' Dr Tripp absently pats Leonard's fair head. 'We must get on. So many patients . . .' He raps on the Bones' front door.

'Little girl.'

Jessie looks up. Then she scrambles to her feet and runs to the gate.

'Me, my lady?'

It's Lady Emily. She's gazing down at Jessie over the hedge with sad eyes under her broad-brimmed grey hat.

'I have come to enquire about your sister. I believe she —'

'Yes, my lady.' Jessie backs away. They say Lady Emily has gone a bit queer since her son, Mr Raymond, was killed in the war. 'I'll tell Father.'

Lady Emily comes through the gate. 'I've been blackberrying. Look.' She holds up a basket. Her soft grey boots are caked with mud. 'Such beauties this year.'

She raises her voice. 'Good morning, Dr Tripp.'

The doctor lifts his hat. 'Lady Emily.'

He knocks again at the door. 'We'd better go round to the back,' he says to Harold. 'Mr Bone seems —'

'No, sir, I can hear him coming.'

Then the door is pulled open, and Jessie's stomach turns to ice and she stands still in the middle of the path. For she sees that Father is having to support himself against the door frame, and that his face is the colour of dust.

'Father?' Frank's voice is hoarse. 'What's the matter, Father?'

Father turns his head. He says, 'Mrs Kellaway —' and then he clears his throat.

'No – Don't say it . . .' Mrs Kellaway lets go of Leonard and starts forward blindly. 'She's never gone, Mr Bone. That lovely girl . . . She's been like a little mother ever since your poor wife passed away . . .'

Father gives a quick nod, cutting her off. 'She's at rest. 'Tis God's will. I'd be grateful, Mrs Kellaway, if you'd show Dr Tripp upstairs. I must talk to the children.'

Jessie finds that Minna is by her side, holding on tightly to her arm. She sees the doctor and Mrs Kellaway squeeze past Father and hears their footsteps mount the stairs. Now they're in the room with Alice, she thinks. They're speaking to her. They're making her sit up again and talk. That's what they're doing.

But now Father's coming down the path towards her, steering Harold and a white-faced Frank, and little Leonard is there too, already tearful, and Father's speaking, and Jessie's mind can't hold on any longer to the good pictures of Alice that she wants to hold on to, and instead she's having to hear the words – the awful, unbearable words – that tell her she'll never again in her whole life be able to tell Alice anything.

Everyone seems to be talking; crying.

Only eight-year-old Jessie is tearless. She stands with her

father and her brothers, silent and bereft, seeing nothing and hearing nothing.

Almost nothing. Just two things.

One is Father, looking down at her as only Father can, his eyes demanding that she hear him and that she take notice.

'Jessie must be our little mother now.'

Gently he pushes Leonard forward, and the small boy clings to Jessie's skirt and buries his face.

'Oh, Father, I'll try.' Now it will be Jessie who sits in Alice's chair at Friday night supper, in charge of the housekeeping purse.

'A little mother to us all.'

And, almost forgotten on the edge of the little group, Lady Emily, standing with her blackberry basket, saying over and over again, 'I am so very sorry, Bone. I am so very, very sorry.'

Chapter Two

We've done it, Joanna thought. We've moved into Violet Bottom.

Well, nearly.

She lifted the last two dresses from her suitcase and hung them in the wardrobe, next to her brand-new school uniform. The rest of her clothes were going to have to stay where they were for the moment. There wasn't much hanging space. Not much space of any kind, come to that.

She perched on the edge of the bed and surveyed the room. It was sure to look bigger once everything was tidied away. Probably it was the sloping ceiling that made it seem so small; that, and the faded wallpaper of heavy blue and white stripes. It would look different all painted white, or with a few posters up or something.

But she was glad she'd chosen this bedroom. The other one, at the back, had a fireplace, and a fire might be quite fun on a cold night, but hers had the view. She remembered the view from when the estate agent had shown them round the cottage back in December. She crossed to the window. The front garden didn't look too good, no more than a stretch of rough grass and one or two ragged bushes at the moment, but beyond that she saw the rise and fall of fields and hedges and far misty hills; half the county of Dorset seemed to be stretched out in front of her.

It was very quiet. Nothing moved except a few black and white cows grazing in the field across the lane, and a tiny plane, trailing its thin white vapour line so high in the sky that no sound came from it at all. Almost, it was too quiet.

Their London house, roomy and comfortable, that Joanna had lived in all her life until now, had stood in a leafy suburb, but even so there'd been the ever-present rumble of traffic in the air that is the background to life for every Londoner. Buses had passed the end of the road, and the tube station had been only five minutes away. Violet Bottom was going to take some getting used to.

'It's worth it, though.' She almost spoke the words out loud, catching sight of herself in the mirror, a quite short, brown-eyed girl with fair hair pulled back into a single plait, dressed in an orange shirt and old jeans. 'I'm glad we came.'

There just hadn't been anything else to do. Not once Corinne had come into their lives . . .

'Jo . . . I'm going down to make some coffee. Want some?'

Joanna went out on to the tiny landing.

'Just look at this bath.' Hilary pointed with her cleaning cloth. 'How do you think it got into this state?'

'Perhaps the last owners never used it,' Joanna suggested. 'Probably they went outside and rolled in a stream.'

'Oh, sure.' Hilary led the way down the steep, narrow stairs. 'Dead rural. At least someone put a bath in at some point. No tub in front of the fire for us.'

She filled the kettle at the sink and looked round for somewhere to plug it in. Every surface in the kitchen was stacked high with plates and cups and frying pans and saucepans; with cartons of milk and cereal and sugar and pasta.

'Goodness knows where it's all going to be stowed away. There's only that little larder place. I should never have let Dad have the fridge.'

'We'll get it sorted out.' Joanna had gone through into the little living room.

'I couldn't have been thinking very straight.'

'Maybe not.' She squeezed past the furniture that the removal men had set down haphazardly all over the room and picked up the envelope lying on the table.

Joanna Milford, 2 Violet Bottom, Lansbury Abbas, Dorset . . .

That proves it, she thought. We really live here now. We don't live in London any longer. London's a hundred miles away. Dad and Patrick are a hundred miles away. We're on our own.

She didn't know whether to feel triumphant or frightened.

The envelope had been one of several on the mat when they arrived. The card inside said GOOD LUCK IN YOUR NEW HOME, and there was a picture of a bright pink hippopotamus sitting in a rocking chair with its feet up on the mantelpiece. Half a dozen of her London school friends had scrawled their signatures inside: Steve, Claire, Paula, Ziggy . . . Paula Rossi had been her best friend. And Steve – well, Steve had been a bit special.

'Coffee, love.'

'Thanks.'

She stood the card up on the window sill next to the one from Gran – Hilary's mother – which showed a thatched cottage with smooth green lawns and bluebirds flying overhead.

'Yuk.' Hilary grinned, looking at it. 'How terribly *not* like Violet Bottom.' She glanced out of the window at the shaggy, knee-high grass and weeds. 'Nobody's ever going to put this place on a card or a calendar.'

'They might,' Joanna said. 'One day.'

Hilary shook her head. 'Anyway, it was kind of her to send it, considering –'

They sippped their coffee in silence.

Considering how unhappy she is about Mum and Dad splitting up, Joanna finished the sentence in her head. About the four of us living in two different halves – Mum and me, Dad and Patrick. But it was the best way, Gran. Really it was. Mum was determined to get away. I couldn't let her go on her own, could I? And in the end, I was glad to go. It was such a mess.

Hilary had picked up one of her letters again and was frowning over it. Joanna could see it was from her solicitor. She put down her mug.

'I think I'll go and look at the garden.'

'Don't get cold, then. It's only April, remember.'

It was certainly blustery. Joanna walked down to the little front gate, half off its hinges, and stood looking at the mud lane and the swirling tyre treads left by their removal van. Really, 'track' would be a better word than lane. There wasn't another house within sight, except for their 'other half', Number One, Violet Bottom.

It was nearly a mile to the road, and then another mile to the village of Lansbury Abbas. She and Mum had measured it that morning on the milometer as they bounced over the potholes in Mum's old Fiat, stacked up to the roof with suitcases and boxes and pot plants.

She breathed in lungfuls of air, watching the big white clouds scudding across the blue sky.

Why did people have to behave in such a stupid way? So selfishly? They'd been a perfectly happy, ordinary family until Corinne had come along and broken it all up.

No, not fair. It was Dad who chose to break everything up.

He'd always been very friendly and free and easy with his students at the college where he was a lecturer. Too free and easy, Mum said. Mum herself was a physiotherapist, and liked things orderly and tidy and organised. Dad was different; he'd invite a bunch of students round to the house and put on some music and have a drink with them. No wonder they all seemed to admire him. Corinne, with her frizzy sand-coloured hair, her green eyes and her freckled arms bare under her blue denim waistcoat seemed no different from any other nineteen-year-old student. To start with.

It was a long time before Joanna noticed that Dad had begun coming home late in the evenings, saying he'd been at a meeting or a lecture at college. By the time she did notice, it was too late.

Somehow – and she never dared ask Mum how she'd found out – everything had come out into the open. Apparently Dad had been meeting Corinne all this time. And worse. Much worse. He was going to move in with her, in to her scruffy little flat above a launderette just down the road from the college.

And he'd done it. Left them all and gone to live with Corinne instead.

Joanna sighed, remembering.

Then she turned and walked back up the path. Forget it. The future was what mattered now.

She looked at the pair of cottages. Mum was right; they were never going to get on a calendar. They weren't pretty thatched dwellings with their gardens full of flowers. They weren't even particularly old. They were simply shabby brick cottages whose tiled roofs were covered in moss.

Looked at from the front like this, their cottage – Number Two – was the left-hand half of the pair. Over the years, things had been done to it: a rather rickety porch had been built around the front door; the door itself had a glass panel in it and was painted a glossy black; their living room window had been enlarged and double-glazed.

Nothing seemed to have been done to the other cottage. No porch, no double glazing, no fresh paint. It seemed simply to have stood there since it was built, unchanged behind its grubby net curtains.

The only sign that someone did indeed live there was the front garden. Unlike theirs, it had been carefully dug and raked and planted with neat rows of cabbages and fruit bushes.

'Hello.' Hilary opened the front door. 'Found any violets?'

'Not yet. But there must be some, otherwise why call it Violet Bottom?'

'Good question.'

They searched the front grass, then walked along by the hedge on the far side, still looking.

'Celandines.' Hilary pointed. 'Primroses. Two daffodils, rather windswept. Will they do?'

'If we don't find any violets, let's sue someone. Wrongly named cottage.'

They strolled round to the back.

'Well stocked,' said Joanna, glancing at her mother hopefully. 'Mature.'

'It's dreadful,' said Hilary. 'Dreadful, Jo.'

The garden stretched into the distance, climbing steadily. It was a tangle of trees, ivy, brambles and nettles. Near where they stood an old shed had rotted and collapsed, and someone had had a bonfire, leaving a scattering of charred wood and newspaper and broken bricks.

'Why did I let you talk me into buying this cottage? It's quite unsuitable.'

'No, really,' said Joanna. 'It's lovely. So's this garden. Or it will be.'

'You're joking.'

'Eventually.' She touched a branch. 'I bet this is an apple tree. Or a plum or something. Just think, our own fruit.'

'Eventually.'

Joanna trod down a few brambles. 'We might find anything under all this lot. Things like . . .'

She stood still, then dropped to her knees.

'Hey, Mum. Come and look.'

Hilary came over. 'Jo, mind. That could be next door's garden there.'

Joanna shook her head. 'No, I'm sure it's on our side.

Look at this.' She tugged at the brambles and ivy. Underneath was a heavy slab of wood, balanced on a low square wall of faded brick.

'I should keep away from there if I was you.'

They looked round, startled. A white-haired old man was gazing at them steadily. He wore a collarless shirt and an old black waistcoat, and was leaning on a spade.

'Oh . . . Good morning.' Hilary took a step towards him, smiling nervously. 'I hope we haven't encroached on to your side. It's a bit difficult to see the boundary until we've tamed this lot.' She gestured at the garden.

'Ah. Take you a year or two, that will, the state it's in.'

'Yes, well . . . We're already making plans.' She appealed to Joanna. 'Aren't we, darling?'

Joanna scrambled to her feet. 'You won't know it soon,' she assured him.

The old man gave a wheezing cough and nodded. 'They all says that.'

'Do they?' asked Joanna. 'Who?'

'The folk that move in there.' He coughed again.

'In our house, do you mean?'

'They'm all alike. Full of it at the beginning . . . Going to do this and that . . . Next you know, they'm off again, and a new lot's in. None of them don't stay no length of time.'

Hilary said, 'You've been here a long time yourself, have you, Mr – ?'

'Bone,' said the old man. 'Leonard . . .' He was overtaken with another coughing fit. 'Leonard Bone.'

'I'm Hilary Milford.' She half held out her hand, and then dropped it again. 'Joanna, my daughter.'

'Hi,' said Joanna. 'We've just moved down from London.'

He nodded, making no comment, going on standing there, seemingly in no hurry.

Finally he said, 'Me whole life.'

'Sorry?'

20

'I lived here me whole life. Born in this cottage, I was. We all was. Up in our front bedroom.'

'Goodness,' said Hilary. 'Were you a large family, Mr Bone?'

He pulled a crumpled pack from his back pocket, and took out a cigarette. 'Middling,' he said.

'Our cottage seems quite a squash,' Joanna volunteered. 'And there are only two of us.'

He was striking match after match, trying to light the cigarette against the wind. He looked at her.

'Two?' he said. He blew out smoke and coughed again. 'We was a bit more'n that.'

'Were you?'

He took a step nearer her, counting on his fingers.

'Father and Mother, o' course. Though Mother passed away when I was born. Alice . . . the oldest. She went in the flu epidemic at the end of the Great War . . .'

'Oh dear.' Hilary shuffled uncomfortably. 'You've had some tragedies, Mr Bone.'

'Same as most folks.' He went on counting. 'Harold.' Another finger went down. 'Then Frank.'

He paused.

'Then you?' Joanna guessed.

'That's right.' He put the last finger down. 'The youngest.' He gave a wheezy laugh. 'The babby of the family.'

'Was that your only sister?' Joanna asked. 'The one that died? Alice?'

He turned away. 'The only one,' he said.

'That must have been really sad.'

'T'was a long time ago,' he said shortly.

'Yes, I know,' said Joanna. 'How old was she?'

'Jo –' Hilary touched her arm. 'I'm sure Mr Bone wants to get on. And we must, too. There's such a lot to do . . .'

'Ah,' said the old man, walking away. 'They all says that.'

Chapter Three

For the rest of the day, Joanna and Hilary scrubbed floors, washed shelves, shifted furniture, unpacked, sorted. The work was far from finished when Joanna glanced up and realised that it was getting dark.

'Enough,' said Hilary. 'Stop, Jo.' She looked round and shivered. 'Let's get the fire going.'

'OK.' Joanna looked round. 'What with, exactly?'

'Oh, I don't know.'

Clearly through the partition wall they could hear the signature tune for a television chat show and a burst of applause. Somewhere in the background, a bird was chattering.

'I thought that old chap was a bit deaf,' groaned Hilary. 'And it sounds like a budgie of all things. You can hear every sound through these walls. Oh, this is no good. Come on, let's go out.'

They locked up. Outside, the darkness engulfed them. They had to grope their way to the car.

'A torch,' said Hilary. 'I'll buy one tomorrow.'

They bumped along the dark lane. Joanna kept her eyes fixed on the distant line of orange lights that marked the main road.

It wasn't till they were settled in the snug, low-ceilinged bar of the Partridge Inn in Lansbury Abbas that she began to relax. There was a hubbub of friendly country voices and a darts match was going on in one corner. They found a quiet table and the landlady brought them homemade beef casserole.

Joanna sat back.

'Dorset,' she said. 'We've got here.'

They might have gone anywhere. Mum hadn't minded where they went as long as it was a long way from London. Once Dad had moved out, the house sold, the money split between them, and divorce proceedings started, all she'd wanted to do was get away.

She'd applied for physiotherapy jobs all over the country – Cornwall, Liverpool, Scotland – but only the Dorset application was successful. So that was where she'd go. Joanna remembered her coming back from the interview, happy and excited, and sitting at the kitchen table to tell Patrick and her all about it.

'It'll mean new schools, of course, darlings. But that's no problem. Nice country schools, think of that. No more big city hassle.' She'd stretched. 'Oh, it'll be good to get away. A fresh start for all three of us.'

She smiled at Joanna.

'Remember that film we saw on TV the other night? *Far from the Madding Crowd*? We'll be in real Thomas Hardy country.'

'Thomas Hardy?' seventeen-year-old Patrick said. 'I don't fancy that. I like big city hassle. All my friends are here.'

'But, Patrick, you'll – '

'What about my A-levels?'

'You could do them at another school. Or a college.'

'No thanks, Mum.' Patrick was always polite. 'I'll stay here if you don't mind.'

'Here? But the house has been sold.'

'With Dad.'

There was silence.

'Dad?' Joanna had said at last. 'With Dad and – her?'

'Not in that flat, Patrick,' Hilary said in a tight voice.

'They won't be in that flat much longer. Dad's buying a better one now the money's come through, a bigger one. I can move in with them if I want to. I asked him. It's OK, it's only for a year till I leave school.'

Joanna, watching her mother's face, could hardly bear it.

'Darlings, we've always said you can decide for yourselves. Jo, if you'd rather be with Dad as well . . .'

Joanna had crossed over to sit on the arm of her chair.

'No,' she'd said. 'Of course not. I'll go to Dorset with you.' And she'd gone on sitting there even after Patrick had left the room and closed the door quietly behind him . . .

'Jo?'

With a start, Joanna returned to the present.

'Your food's getting cold, love.'

'Sorry.'

They ate in silence.

'Jo,' Hilary said at last. 'I know I shouldn't say this, but do you think it'll be all right? New school tomorrow? New job? Do you think we've been stupid?'

'No, I don't,' said Joanna. 'I think we're doing the right thing. And so do you, Mum.'

Hilary smiled at her. 'Let's have some lemon meringue pie,' she said. 'One portion and two spoons.'

But back in the cottage that night, lying awake in the little front bedroom, listening to the old man, Leonard Bone, moving about as he went to bed next door, Joanna felt a tremor of fear as her mother's words came back to her.

New school tomorrow.

'It'll be all right,' she said to herself, turning over. 'Perfectly all right. I expect it'll be good fun.'

Chapter Four

As they were climbing the stairs, a bell began to shrill over their heads.

'Don't worry,' the teacher shouted cheerfully over the din. 'There isn't really a fire. Nearly there now.'

He swerved to the left along yet another corridor and Joanna followed, breathless, trying to keep a firm grip on her school bag and the handful of timetables and course details she'd just been given. From one of the windows, she caught a glimpse of the blue Fiat disappearing down the drive. Her mother was hurrying off to start her own first day at work.

'You'll soon be used to it all.'

'Yes.'

It was very much larger than her old school. She supposed that when she'd started there she'd probably felt a bit lost or bewildered. If so, she'd forgotten it long ago. All her friends had been starting as well.

This time there was only her. There wouldn't be a single person here that she knew. And it wasn't even the beginning of term. The summer term had started a week ago.

'Here you go.' The teacher pushed open a door. 'This is your tutor group.'

The room seemed very full. Most of the girls were wearing trousers. Joanna, who had agonised that morning over what to wear, had finally chosen the navy skirt.

The tutor, Mrs Greenhill, greeted her and wrote her name and address in the register.

'Right – Lansbury Abbas. So you'll be travelling on one of the school buses every day?'

'Yes,' said Joanna. 'My mother drove me in this morning, but –'

'Fine. Now –' Mrs Greenhill looked round the room. 'Who's going to look after Joanna? Show her where her classes are and so on?'

Her glance fell on a girl in the back corner, a girl with short streaky blonde hair. 'Vivien? You live in Lansbury Abbas. I'm talking to you, Vivien Dennis.'

The girl looked up. 'Shut up, Paul. It's Paul, Mrs Greenhill. He's telling us about this video he saw last night.'

'That's enough. Look, here's a seat, Joanna.' Mrs Greenhill was steering her to Vivien's table. 'Make room, Becky.'

A tall girl with a mass of curly dark hair turned to smile at Joanna, and moved her bag so that she could sit down.

'Now,' said Mrs Greenhill, 'we must get on. Vivien, make sure Joanna has everything she needs.'

Vivien nodded, picking at her mauve-varnished finger nails.

Mrs Greenhill started talking about a school skiing trip that was going to happen after Christmas.

No chance of that, Joanna thought. Far too expensive now. Besides, I wouldn't know anyone.

The boy called Paul leaned forward.

'Everything she needs, eh?' He pressed his chin down on the end of a ruler until it bent into a tight curve. 'I could give her everything she needs, couldn't I, Viv?'

Vivien Dennis gave him a push. 'Shut up, I keep telling you. Ignore him, Joanne. We all do.'

Lessons are lessons.

On that first day, Joanna let herself drop gratefully into the somehow comforting routine, going to whichever room Vivien indicated, taking the books she was given, doing her best with the work.

There was maths. She'd been put in the top set and, although they were using an unfamiliar syllabus, she coped.

There was biology. A few problems here, but the teacher kept her back at the end of the lesson to help sort things out.

That took up most of Break. There was no time to have anything to eat or drink, even if she'd known where such things could be found. After Break came French, which Joanna found easy. And then, just before lunch, there was PE.

'Hurry up, Joanne.' Vivien was waiting impatiently to take her to the sports hall. 'It's basketball today.'

Joanna's heart sank. She'd never played basketball in her life. With some misgiving she changed with the rest of the girls into her new red T-shirt and navy shorts, and went through into the hall.

Boys were there as well as girls. At her old school, the sexes had been separated for sports. She walked slowly round the edge of the hall, eyeing everyone uncertainly. They all seemed completely at ease, milling about and laughing, sure of themselves.

'Right.' The teacher in charge blew his whistle. He had a thick black moustache and was wearing a maroon and white track suit. 'Skills practice for five minutes. Then we'll make the teams up. Find a partner. Quickly.'

Joanna took a tentative step forward.

'Space out. One standing here.' The teacher pointed. 'The other one across there . . .'

She saw Vivien grab the hand of a tall boy with fair hair and glasses.

'Richie, darling. Your lucky day.'

He pulled away angrily. Vivien ran off laughing to pair up with Paul instead. Everyone was finding a partner now. Everyone except her.

'Ready?' The teacher had a ball in his hand, three more

at his feet. 'You're going to –'

He broke off, staring at Joanna, stranded in the centre of the hall. 'Come on, dear. Where's your partner? You're holding everyone up.'

'Sorry. I –'

He looked at her more closely. 'Do I know you?'

She shook her head. 'No, I don't expect . . .'

'Name?'

She told him. He made her spell her surname. She felt everyone staring at them now, listening.

'Oh, you're *new*.' He sighed heavily. 'Why does nobody tell me these things? Well, you'd better just watch this one, dear, if you haven't got a partner.'

'I'll sit out, Mr Sharman.' The girl called Becky started forward, pulling a small, black-haired girl with her. 'Then Leela can be her partner.'

'Just wait till you're asked,' the teacher said. 'Thank you so much, Becky love.'

Becky flushed and stepped back again.

'Ah-ha.' Mr Sharman pounced. 'Don't think, lad, I can't see you there, alone and palely loitering. A beanpole like you.'

It was the boy in glasses that Vivien had called Richie.

'Your partner,' said Mr Sharman to Joanna. 'Richard Horsefield. The answer to a maiden's prayer.'

Vivien and Paul laughed. The boy stood by Joanna silently, hands hanging at his sides, his face turned away. She felt a sudden hot spurt of dislike for him, for Mr Sharman, for everything and everyone in this school.

'Right, exactly like last week.' Mr Sharman ran back a few paces and aimed one of the balls, ready to throw it to the first pair. 'Now wake up, the whole lot of you.'

At last it was lunchtime.

As Joanna ate her packed lunch, she tried not to think about the PE session. Richard had gone through the skills practice without once speaking to her or looking at her. Then he'd been put in one of the teams and Joanna, hopelessly out of her depth, had sat on the sidelines and watched.

Rather to her surprise, Richard played neatly and accurately, though more as if the game was a problem he wanted to solve than as if he cared whether his team won or lost. She could see that Vivien and her friends were spending quite a lot of their time teasing him; trying to upset him. He ignored them completely. In fact, by the end, she still hadn't seen him exchange a word with anyone.

'All right, Joanna?' Her tutor, Mrs Greenhill, went past as she finished her sandwiches. 'Are they looking after you?'

'Oh, yes. Thank you.'

As they finished eating, people wandered away in pairs or groups. Joanna took her stuff back to her locker and spent a long time packing it away tidily.

'Outside.' Sixth-formers were patrolling the corridors, searching the classrooms and cloakrooms. 'Everyone outside. No hanging around in here.'

'Get lost, you –'

It was Vivien Dennis and her friends further along the corridor, arguing and swearing as they were pushed towards the outside door. 'I'll get you, Darren Humphries. Wait till I see you down the –'

'Out.'

Joanna was pushed out with the rest. She hung about on the fringes of Vivien's little crowd, not knowing what else to do.

'I'll smash his face in, that Darren Humphries.'

'Thinks he's –'

Joanna's own face ached, trying to look interested and amused and ready to join in. They drifted across the field, shouting and pushing each other around.

'Shut up, Viv. You know you fancy him.'

'Joanne!' Vivien turned round to shout into the wind. 'Come on, Joanne.'

At least she'd noticed her. Joanna hurried to catch them up.

'Bloody awful place. Isn't it, Joanne?'

'Actually –' she said.

They turned and stared at her.

'It's Joanna.' She tried to smile as she said it. 'My name. Or Jo, I suppose. But not Joanne.'

Two of the boys laughed. Vivien's blue-green eyes flicked over her and then lost interest.

'Please yourself,' she said. 'Come on, you lot.'

They walked away towards the cycle sheds. This time, she didn't try to follow them.

'Oh, Jo-Jo,' one of the boys called back. 'Want to come down the boozer with me tonight, Jo-Jo?'

She walked round the field once; then again. She passed Richard, sitting alone on a bench, but he didn't look up. The second time, she glimpsed the headphones in his ears and realised he was listening to music.

It seemed a very long time until the bell finally summoned them all indoors again.

The afternoon was better.

'Welcome, Joanna.' The history teacher, Mr Rawlinson, was warm and friendly. 'I'll show you what we've been doing.'

It was a project about changes in the twentieth century. The walls of the room were covered in photographs and newspaper cuttings. Some recruiting posters of the First World War said *The Women of Britain Say GO!* and *Your Country Needs YOU.*

'The war affected everyone. Millions of men went to fight, and often didn't come back. And there were new inventions, and new ideas and then another war came looming up. People have lived through so much . . .'

He shook his head.

'I know it sounds high-powered stuff. But we're concentrating on just one small part of Dorset, a really traditional area, where life used to centre completely on the Big House and its estate. We're working in small groups, looking at newspapers, interviewing people and so on, finding out how life used to be and how it's changed. OK?'

Joanna nodded.

'I'm putting you into a group that really needs your help. They're only two of them because someone's dropped out. They're going to interview an old lady who used to be a servant at Ennington Hall, the Big House.'

Perhaps I'll make some friends here, Joanna thought, following him across the room. Then she saw who the two members of her group were. Vivien Dennis and Richard Horsefield.

'All three from Lansbury Abbas. So you'll be able to share your local knowledge.' Mr Rawlinson smiled round at them. 'Now, the interview's all set up for a week today. Make sure you explain everything to Joanna, you two.'

He went away. Richard sat fiddling with a tape recorder. Vivien, perched on the table, was chatting to a friend in another group.

Joanna gave up after a while and started reading a 1940s newspaper cutting about Dorset Land Girls bringing in a bumper harvest. After a few minutes, the final bell of the afternoon rang. Her first day at school was over.

Chapter Five

I'll never have to do it again, Joanna thought, gazing out of the bus window at the passing hedges. Tomorrow will be different. Better.

That wouldn't be difficult.

Oh, come on, she told herself. Some of it was all right. Mrs Greenhill wasn't bad. Nor was that biology teacher. And the history project sounded interesting. Sort of.

There was a burst of laughter from the back seat. She didn't need to turn round to know who it came from. Vivien Dennis and her crowd had been shouting and catcalling the whole journey.

'See you, Jonesy, mate.' One of them was getting off. 'Mind how you go tonight. Remember what we told you . . .'

'If you can't be good, be careful . . .'

'What do you know about it, Viv?'

'More than you ever will, Jonesy . . .'

A round-faced boy with ginger hair was swinging his way up to the front of the bus. He stopped by Joanna.

'Not as much as she does, I bet.' He turned his head to grin at Vivien. He wasn't looking at Joanna at all. 'Isn't that so, Jo-Jo?'

Every day, she thought, wearily. Morning and afternoon, I've got to be cooped up in here with them.

The bus slowed down and stopped.

'Cheers, Jonesy.'

As the boy turned at the door to wave to the back seat, the heavy bag on his shoulder swung round. There were more screams of laughter.

'Whoops. Sorry, mate. Didn't see you there.'

'Rub it better, Richie.'

'Itchy Richie.'

The bus started again. It overtook Jonesy, gesturing to Vivien and the rest of the back seat, and sped on. Ahead of them Joanna saw the church tower and rooftops of Lansbury Abbas.

She looked at Richard. If the blow on the head had hurt him, he gave no sign. He'd picked up his glasses and readjusted his headphones, and was sitting in the front seat as he'd sat the whole journey, gazing straight ahead of him.

What's the matter with him, she thought, irritated in spite of herself. They treat him like dirt and all he can do is sit there with those stupid things in his ears.

'Picadilly Circus. Everybody out,' shouted the bus driver. Joanna seized her bag and hurried to the door. 'Especially you at the back,' he added.

Vivien came rushing to the door, calling something to her friends, and pushed past Joanna. The driver nodded at her retreating blonde head.

'Not much like a church rector's daughter, is she?'

Joanna laughed. 'No,' she said, and jumped down to the road.

The bus went away. They were by the War Memorial in the middle of Lansbury Abbas. She drew a deep breath of fresh air.

'She is, actually.'

Joanna turned round. 'What?'

'Vivien,' said Richard. For once he'd put away his stereo. 'The Rector's daughter. Look.'

They watched Vivien walk down a footpath towards the church, swinging her bag from hand to hand, and go into a house at the far end.

'Rectors' daughters aren't like that,' said Joanna.

'That's stereotyping,' said Richard.

What was he talking about? Stereos? Stereotyping? At

least he'd spoken to her.

The church clock began to strike five. Joanna sat down on the War Memorial step to wait for her mother.

It was peaceful there. The traffic was all out on the bypass, and the village itself was so quiet she could hear birds singing in the churchyard. Across the street was a house called The Old School. You could still see traces of the village school it had once been: enormous high windows and the clear shape of a playground in the front. Next door to it two women stood chatting outside the village shop. A dog barked. A car went past.

An old man came out of the shop, carrying several paper bags and a bunch of daffodils. He stowed the bags into the basket of an old bicycle leaning against a wall and Joanna saw that it was Leonard Bone, their new neighbour.

He wheeled the bicycle carefully across the street and touched his cap to her.

'Turned out nice.'

'Yes, yes, it has.'

'Cold at nights, mind.' He propped the bicycle against the step. 'I've put you some logs through.'

She twisted round to look up at him. 'What? Sorry . . .'

'Logs,' he said. 'I put some through into your garden this morning. You'll be wanting a fire.'

'Oh,' said Joanna. 'Thank you very much, Mr Bone.'

He nodded. 'You stopping there long?'

'Till my mother picks me up. She'll be here in a minute.'

'Keep an eye on me bike, then,' he said. 'I'm going down the grave with these daffs.'

'Oh, right,' said Joanna. She hesitated. 'Is it your sister's grave, Mr Bone? Alice?'

He coughed. 'Her and Mother and Father. They'm all in together. 'Tis Father's birthday today, look.'

'I see.'

She watched him go. Leonard Bone himself looked about eighty; hard to imagine his father.

And Alice, who'd died so long ago of the flu? She'd never grown old. Perhaps never even grown up . . .

'Sorry I'm late, Jo.' Her mother was smiling from the car window. 'Get in, darling. I need tea, don't you? How was it at school?'

'OK,' said Joanna. 'I've got to wait a moment. I'm bike-sitting.'

She explained about Mr Bone, and how he'd given them some logs.

'He's a nice old bloke, really,' said Hilary. 'I'm not sure I want to live next door to him, though.'

'I don't mind,' said Joanna. 'I like him being there.' It was so very dark at Violet Bottom: a sea of darkness stretching for miles and miles.

Hilary laughed. 'Would he be any good in an emergency? Look, he's coming back now.'

They drove off, waving to Mr Bone as they went. The sun was shining and the gardens were bright with flowers and the night seemed a long way off.

'Was it all right, Mum?' Joanna asked. 'Your day?'

'Oh, fine,' said Hilary. 'Quite a good set-up really. Nice patients. I did three arthritic knees and a couple of whiplash injuries.'

She turned to look at Joanna. 'What about you, love?'

'OK,' Joanna said. 'It was . . .' She couldn't think of anything to say about it all. 'It was OK,' she finished.

'That's good.'

They drove on, not talking. On their left was a long stone wall, enclosing some sort of parkland. After a while they passed some large ornamental gates standing wide open, with a driveway leading away through an avenue of trees. A large notice said: ENNINGTON COUNTRY PARK. Perhaps this had once been the Big House that Mr Rawlinson had mentioned.

'Jo?'

'Yes?'

'You will tell me, won't you, darling, if –'

'If what?'

'You know . . .' Hilary hesitated. 'If you're missing Dad or anything. You know what I mean.'

'I'm not,' said Joanna. 'I'm not missing him.'

'Oh,' said Hilary. She overtook a van. 'Well, anyway,' she said, 'he'll be keeping in touch, like we agreed.'

'Yes.'

The car turned into the beginning of the lane. To save herself from thinking about anything else, Joanna thought about the history project.

It might be quite fun, even with Richard and Vivien. This interview they were going to do with the old lady could be interesting. The old lady who'd once been a servant at Ennington Hall. What was her name?

Oh, yes. She remembered now. Miss Minna Kellaway.

Chapter Six

Miss Minna Kellaway was very small.

Perhaps it was in contrast to Richard. He towered over her in the narrow hallway. He and Vivien and Joanna flattened themselves against the wall as she turned herself and her walking frame round and led them into her front room.

'Fancy your teacher driving you out here this afternoon in that minibus just to see me.' She lowered herself into a chair by the window, her blue eyes bright, her face flushed and smiling. There seemed no more substance to her than a sparrow. 'Is he going to pick you up again?'

Vivien shook her head. 'He's got some other people to take round, Miss Kellaway. We'll make our own way home.' Vivien was like a different person in here, Joanna thought. It was a week now since she'd started at the school and this was a Vivien she hadn't seen before. Very subdued and polite. 'We all live out this way, you see.'

Mr Rawlinson had explained all this to Miss Kellaway only a few minutes earlier. Perhaps she forgot things quickly or was a bit deaf or something.

The old lady darted a glance at Vivien. 'I seen you before, dear. In the church, weren't it?'

'Could have been.' Vivien flushed. 'A long time ago.'

'The rector's daughter.' Miss Kellaway nodded to herself. 'You was a little tiddler then, but I don't never forget a face. I can see you now, in your little pink frock . . .'

Joanna flicked an eyebrow at Richard. She didn't dare look at Vivien.

'I'll just fix the microphone, Miss Kellaway,' said Richard. She eyed it doubtfully as Vivien turned to the list of questions and Joanna picked up her clipboard. Vivien had told Joanna to take notes, saying that Richard would probably forget to switch the tape recorder on or something.

'Can you tell us about when you started work at Ennington Hall? How old were you . . . ? What sort of work was it . . . ?'

The old lady needed little prompting; plainly she loved talking about her life. Joanna wrote and wrote until her hand ached.

'I went to the Big House as housemaid when I left school in – what? – 1924. My dad had worked on the estate for Sir Wilfred, see, and Mother had worked there once, too. Still did, when they had guests in. So we'd always been connected to the family.'

'How old were you?'

'Fourteen. Glad to go, too. See, Dad had come home from the war – the first war – all smashed up. He weren't never the same after that, though Sir Wilfred kept him on, of course. But he died after a couple of years, and we was left.'

She sighed.

'Mother always said they ought to have put Dad's name on the War Memorial in the village, seeing what the war'd done to him. But they didn't.'

'So you went to Ennington Hall?'

'That's right. School weren't much use to me. I wanted to get out and help my mother. 'Twas hard, mind, in them days. We slept up in the attics and we got up at six – earlier if they had a house party staying. All the grates to do first, cleaning them with blackleading, and laying the fires. Then jugs of hot water to carry up to the bedrooms, the slops to empty . . .'

'Slops?'

Her birdlike glance went from Vivien to Joanna. 'Couldn't have ladies and gentlemen emptying their own slops, could you? I didn't mind. I was young. That's the sort of thing you expect when you're young.'

Her face softened. 'And they was wonderful to work for. Everybody said the same. Sir Wilfred . . . Lady Emily . . . She were a duke's daughter, you know. They was real gentry. You don't get people like that no more.'

Joanna looked at her twisted hands, resting on her walking frame as she talked about the gentry, of their weekend shooting parties on the big estate, of dances and treasure hunts for the young people and their friends, and of the servants who worked for them: the housemaids and parlourmaids and gamekeepers. It was a whole world that had passed, one that was fading away with the old people who'd lived in it.

'Didn't you work terribly long hours?'

She smiled. 'No, no. I had every other Sunday off. And an afternoon off each week. Wonderful. I used to walk over to Mother's for tea, do a bit of washing for her, maybe, and walk back. Nice little walk that was when the weather was fine, down to Violet Bottom and back . . .'

'Violet Bottom?' Joanna looked up. 'You lived at Violet Bottom? Which house?'

'Number Two. That's where I were born.'

'That's where I live,' said Joanna. 'In your old cottage. Isn't that –'

'Shh.' Richard was pointing to the tape, still running.

'Sorry.' Joanna went back to taking notes. Miss Kellaway went on talking about the old days.

'. . . and the big Christmas party. That was a time to remember. Lady Emily used to stand by the Christmas tree with Miss Pamela, and they'd give out the presents with their own hands. And when I left in 1936 Lady Emily said she'd really miss me. That's what she said. But I had to go . . .'

Joanna glanced at her watch. There couldn't be many more minutes' tape left.

'Mother was sick, see. I had to take care of her. She was heavy to lift, but I had the knack of it. Of course, once I left the job we couldn't stay on at Violet Bottom because the cottage belonged to Sir Wilfred. But he let us stay on till the council found us this bungalow.'

She looked around proudly.

'Oh, it's lovely. We was here right through the second war. I worked in a factory then. And the Big House was full of them evacuees from London. What a time we had in the war. You wouldn't have known the village then. The Yanks was all over the place, getting ready for the invasion, see, ready to go across the Channel and clear out that Hitler. Oh, that were a lively time.'

She sighed. 'Too lively for poor Lady Emily. Poor thing. She were never strong. She passed away at the end of the war. Then Sir Wilfred. And the whole estate went to another gentleman – his second cousin I think it was. And then, a year or two back, it was all sold up and they turned it into this Country Park affair. I don't never go near it now. I couldn't bear to see what they done to it. Not when I remember how it were in the old days . . .'

Her voice faltered. Then picked up with a determined cheerfulness.

'There, I mustn't grumble. Mother passed on, but I'm still here. I got this little bungalow. Me legs don't work so well no more, but I get a lovely nurse in, and a lady comes twice a week with the meals on . . .'

With a gurgle and a click, the tape ended. Miss Kellaway blinked.

'Oh, I have run on. Once I got started . . .'

They assured her that it had all been just right.

'We'll put everything you said on to the computer and print it out.'

'We're going to have an exhibition soon, with all the photos and newspapers, and the stories that people have told us.'

40

'You must come,' Joanna said. 'It'll remind you of the old days.'

Miss Kellaway looked doubtful. 'My legs . . .'

'Oh, do come,' said Joanna. 'Look, Richard's got his file here. Has it got any photos or things she could see, Richard?'

Richard tipped the contents of the file on to the table. Miss Kellaway exclaimed over the photographs in delight.

'That's Sir Wilfred as a boy. And that's Mr Raymond before he went off to the trenches. Went off and never come back. That's what turned Lady Emily – well – a bit strange. It broke her heart, see. Just broke her heart.'

She bent over another picture. 'Miss Pamela on her pony. Pretty as a picture, weren't she?'

'And look at this, Miss Kellaway.'

Richard laid a newspaper cutting in front of her. 'It's you. A picture of you.'

'Me?'

'A long time ago. It was a story in the local paper. Back in August 1920.'

The old lady looked at it, bewildered.

'I can't read all that small print. Not without my glasses. What does it say?'

Joanna leaned over her shoulder.

'*THREE LITTLE MAIDS FROM LANSBURY ABBAS*,' she read. '*First prize in the village carnival Fancy Dress competition (11 years and under class) went to this charming trio of local children* – Oh, look. Aren't they sweet?'

The photograph showed two children smiling timidly at the camera, with a smaller child between them holding their hands. All three wore Japanese kimonos tied with wide sashes, and held fans up to their faces.

Joanna went on reading.

'*The surprise for many was that the youngest "little maid" (centre) was, in fact, a little lad – 7-year-old*

Leonard Bone of 1, Violet Bottom, Lansbury Abbas. The others were (left) Minna Kellaway (10) of 2, Violet Bottom, and her friend Jessie Bone (right), also 10, the sister of Leonard.'

Joanna stared at the paper.

'But, Miss Kellaway –'

The old lady was smiling. 'Yes, I recall it now. First prize. Mother made those costumes for us. Wonderful with a needle, my mother. She got the idea from some pictures in a magazine. "Three Little Maids from School" – 'twas a very popular song at the time. Anything Japanese was all the rage. So she sat down and copied the costumes. And made the fans out of paper and we painted them.'

Joanna said, 'But –'

'I still got that fan, after all these years, put away somewhere.'

'Miss Kellaway,' said Joanna. 'That little boy in the picture is Mr Bone next door to us. But who's the other girl? The one on the right?'

Miss Kellaway looked up at Joanna as if seeing her for the first time.

'On the right, dear?'

'It says her name was Jessie Bone,' said Joanna. 'The sister of Leonard. But Mr Bone told me he only had one sister. Her name was Alice, and she died of the flu.'

'He told you that, did he? Then I'm sure he's right. I don't remember nothing more about it.'

'But –'

'So long ago,' said the old lady. ''Tis best left.'

'I only –'

'*Joanne*,' said Vivien. 'Come on.'

Miss Kellaway struggled to her feet. 'You'll have to go now,' she said. 'That teacher's coming back for you.'

'No, we –'

'I'm going to have my rest.' She was urging them out of the room, opening the front door. 'I get very tired.'

Richard was still packing up the tape recorder. 'Thank you, anyway, Miss Kellaway. We'll be writing to you and –'

'No need,' she said. 'You run along now.' And they found themselves out on the doorstep with the door shut behind them.

Rain was falling in a light drizzle. They looked at each other.

'Stupid old bat,' said Vivien. Her usual manner had come straight back. 'Right off her trolley. Come on.'

Joanna glanced back and saw Miss Kellaway's front curtains had been drawn. 'She was fine till the end. I must have upset her.'

'Just the sight of you, I expect, Jo-Jo.'

'The sight of herself, maybe,' Richard put in awkwardly. 'When she was young, sort of thing. And now she's old. Perhaps I shouldn't have shown her that cutting.'

'Quite right, dickhead,' said Vivien. 'All your fault.'

Joanna said nothing. As they walked back through the village it wasn't so much Miss Kellaway that she was thinking of, as the girl that the newspaper had described as her childhood friend. Jessie Bone.

Once Vivien and Richard had both gone off home, Joanna went across to the churchyard. The birds were singing through the rain, and the scent of primroses drifted on the air as she walked over the thick wet grass.

Yes, here it was, with Mr Bone's daffodils wilting a little now:

Sacred to the memory of
LILIAN BONE
beloved wife of George Bone
1880–1913
and of
ALICE
daughter of the above,

died September 11th 1918
aged 14 years.
'Thy Will Be Done'
and of
GEORGE BONE
died May 8th 1965
aged 95 years.
'Peace, perfect peace.'

Joanna pushed back her wet hair from her face. So Alice had been fourteen when she'd died of the flu. The same age as Minna Kellaway when she went to be a housemaid, she thought. The same age as I am now.

One thing was clear. The child in the carnival photograph with Minna and Leonard couldn't be Alice Bone, and just wrongly named 'Jessie' in the text. Alice Bone had been dead nearly two years when that photograph was taken.

Jessie Bone was someone else. Another daughter in the Bone family. Younger sister to Alice, older sister to Leonard.

Why, when Leonard had talked about his family, had he left out all mention of her?

Chapter Seven

It was Sunday afternoon, two days later. Joanna and Hilary were gardening.

'Give me a hand with this a minute, will you?' Hilary called. 'Oh, hurry, Jo, it's slipping –'

'Hang on.' Joanna seized the other end of the heavy branch and helped drag it to one side. 'You'll do your back in if you're not careful.'

Hilary straightened. 'Yes, not funny, a physio with back problems.'

'Not funny, no money coming in. Ow –' She sucked her hand. 'These brambles.'

They stood for a minute, looking at it all.

They'd made a start, that was all you could say. The wood from the collapsing shed had been collected up, and neatly stacked to use as firewood, and they'd cleared most of the rubbish. They'd started on the brambles and ivy, and trimmed back the thick grass and nettles sprouting up everywhere, and even uncovered a rather squashed and ragged patch of what Hilary said were strawberry plants. But the harder they worked the faster it seemed to grow back again.

'If we didn't have to keep stopping and resting . . .'

'If we weren't a couple of lone females . . .'

'Mum . . .' Joanna looked at her accusingly. 'Dad left us, remember? You're going to get a divorce. We're starting a new life.'

'OK,' said Hilary. 'Don't go on, Jo. I know all that.'

'We're much better on our own, Mum.'

Hilary simply nodded. Then she went off to deal with the next fallen branch. Joanna went back to the well.

It had to be a well. There was nothing else it could be.

She hadn't had time to look at it properly that first day, because Mr Bone had interrupted. Now she could.

She knelt down by its low brick edge and cut away the last tough strands of ivy and brambles that grew across the heavy wooden slab. Then she tried to prise it off.

She tugged and tugged but it didn't move. Then she saw that it was fastened down by two heavy metal bolts.

Frustrated, she sat down on the slab. A well was a super thing to find. It could look really nice with crazy paving and flowers round it, the centrepiece of a real old-fashioned cottage garden. Violet Bottom could find itself on a calendar yet.

'Presumably there's still water down there,' Hilary said, coming to look. 'Be useful for watering our vegetables when there's a drought.'

'Vegetables?' scoffed Joanna. 'When?'

'Soon. We'll have to, to save money. Mr Bone offered me some tomato plants only yesterday. We just need to go and ask for them.'

'Ah,' said Joanna. She stood up and brushed herself down. 'I'll go round for them now if you like.'

Nobody answered her knock on Mr Bone's front door, but she could hear the television indoors, and went on round to the back.

Here, there was no need to knock. The back door stood open, leading straight into the living room, and just inside in a patch of sun was Mr Bone in an armchair. A commentator was murmuring his way through a snooker match on the television, and a blue budgerigar was chattering and hopping in a cage in the corner, but Mr Bone was oblivious to both of them. Hands crossed on the newspaper on his lap, spectacles slipping down his face, he was fast asleep, his chin resting on his chest.

Joanna stood there, looking down at his thin thatch of white hair. Each breath that was wheezed in seemed to pause for a second, then was let out again in a little rush.

'Now this shot's going to be . . .' whispered the commentator, 'extremely . . . difficult,' and the bird in the cage clung to the bars of its cage and chirruped in its throat. Joanna tiptoed across the room.

The table still carried the remains of the old man's Sunday lunch, and a teapot with a red cosy on it, but Joanna's attention was elsewhere. She was looking at the photograph on the wall.

It was Alice. Joanna knew that at once. She sat on a high-backed, ornately carved chair, her hands folded in her lap, turned a little away from the camera so that one saw her face in half profile, the mouth soft and faintly smiling, the dark eyes gazing gravely into the distance. Her long straight hair was combed carefully back behind her ears and fastened with a dark ribbon at the back, and this made her look childish, younger than Joanna, while at the same time the high-necked dress with its elaborate tucks and pleats and long sleeves made her seem far older.

Joanna stood for some minutes, looking. And looking at the tiny photograph that had been tucked in at the bottom, a photograph of the Bone family headstone in the churchyard, just as she had seen it on Friday. Only not quite the same. This picture must have been taken soon after Alice's death; her father's name had not yet been added, was not to be added for nearly fifty years. The inscription stopped short with the words: *Thy Will Be Done.*

There were other family photographs on the sideboard. The couple in the faded brown one must be the Bone parents – what were they called? – Lilian and George. They stood stiffly side by side, carefully posed in a photographer's studio, the woman's face shaded by her big hat, her dress reaching to the ground, her arm tucked into her husband's. He was a head taller than her, very upright, dressed in a suit, facing the camera with calm assurance.

There was another, later, picture of a young man in sailor's uniform. No need to guess who this was: scrawled across one corner were the words *All the best, keep smiling, Frank*, and the date *December 1939*. And another, even later, in colour this time, a snapshot of a middle-aged Leonard pushing an old man – surely his father? – along a seaside promenade in a wheelchair.

But it was the largest picture frame that caught Joanna's attention. This held little oval photographs, just head and shoulder portraits, of all the Bone children; Alice at the top, schoolboys Harold and Frank lower down, baby Leonard at the bottom.

Only it wasn't all the children, could not have been, because one of the five ovals – the one just above Leonard – was empty. Someone had taken out the photograph that had once been there. Jessie's photograph, surely . . .

'Oh, and he's done it!' A burst of applause from the television, a trill from the budgerigar and, with a gasp and a jerk of his head, Mr Bone was awake.

'Oh, Mr Bone.' Guiltily, Joanna backed away. 'I've come for the tomato plants.'

His watery blue eyes looked at her steadily.

'Mum told me . . . You were asleep, you see, so I –'

He took off his spectacles, put aside his newspaper and got slowly to his feet. The snooker players were shaking hands now amid a babble of voices. The bird in its cage pecked at its mirror and squawked.

'You pipe down, Billy. He likes the snooker,' the old man remarked, shuffling to the door. 'Football, racing, bit of shouting . . .'

Joanna followed him into the garden. 'Oh, violets,' she exclaimed. They were growing thickly around an outhouse door.

'Always did grow there. They like the damp, I reckon.' He went into the greenhouse. Some of the panes of glass were cracked and the paintwork was peeling. 'This garden can get terribly dry come summer.'

'Yes, I wanted to ask you about that,' said Joanna. 'We've just been looking at the well next door and –'

His head turned sharply.

'I told you,' he said. 'Keep away from that. You won't get no good out of it.'

'I can't lift the cover off. Somebody's bolted it down.'

'There you are then. T'int no use no more.'

He took a tray of plants from a shelf. 'Tell your ma I'll have some marrows later. Don't do eggs no more. I kept hens for nigh on seventy years but I in't got them now. But if she wants some manure for the garden, I knows a chap . . .'

'Mr Bone.' Joanna took a deep breath. 'I've been talking to Miss Kellaway. You know, she used to live in our house . . .'

'Minna?' He sniffed. 'Lot of good that'll do you.'

'. . . about the old days,' she went on doggedly. 'For something we're doing at school. We showed Miss Kellaway a picture of the carnival in 1920. She was dressed up in Japanese costume, and so were you. And there was another girl. The paper said her name was Jessie Bone.'

He shook his head fiercely. 'Don't know nothing about that.' He reached for his cigarettes.

'The newspaper said she was your sister.'

He turned on her. 'You get off home. You in't here five minutes and you –' A spasm of coughing shook him. Joanna backed away.

'Get off home,' he shouted. 'And next time you decide to come round I'll trouble you to wait outside decently, not go poking round my room. You just keep your nose out of other folks' business.'

By the evening, Hilary and Joanna were tired. They sprawled in the little sitting room, Hilary on the sofa and

Joanna in front of the fire, eating their supper on trays and watching *Mastermind*.

'Turn the volume up, Jo,' Hilary said. 'What on earth's Mr Bone doing next door?'

'I don't know.'

They could hear footsteps next door going slowly up and down the stairs; once or twice they seemed to be overhead as if the old man was in his loft. Several times he went out of his front door, and came back in.

'For goodness sake!' Hilary said, after a particularly heavy thud. 'If this is country life, give me a flat in a tower block every time.'

Chapter Eight

Joanna was uneasy. Even after she'd gone to bed, Mr Bone was still moving about, talking to himself and coughing. He'd never sounded as restless as this.

She must go to sleep. Tomorrow was Monday, and the school bus. Tomorrow was Vivien and the others. Tomorrow was PE with Mr Sharman.

Tomorrow was not having any friends.

She cried a little at that, and scolded herself for self-pity. Things would get better. They were bound to.

The tears relaxed her, and she drifted towards sleep. Pictures flitted through her mind, pictures of the journey she used to make each day to her old school – cycling through the leafy roads on a summer morning, calling out to her friends, all of them laughing and talking together . . .

She must have slept because Vivien Dennis was there, and Vivien and some other people were playing in a band. Vivien sat with a huge drum held between her knees and she was beating and banging it. Joanna couldn't stand the noise. She ran and knelt by the drum and tried to wrench the top off it, but it wouldn't come off, it was fastened down. And still the banging went on –

It was real. She sat upright, staring into the dark. Someone was knocking on the wall by her bed.

'Are you there, Missis?' A weak voice, calling.

'Mum –'

A light came on. 'It's all right, Jo. I heard him. I'm going in to see what he wants.'

'Wait for me.'

She pushed her feet into slippers and stumbled down the stairs, took her coat from its peg and followed her mother out into the front garden.

The sky was huge and black, the air stinging cold to her face, driving away the dizziness of sleep. Their slippered feet sank into the grass.

'What do you think he wants, Mum?'

'Don't know. What's that?'

It wasn't a dog; the barking was hollow. Different.

'A fox?'

They groped their way to Mr Bone's front door, and Hilary rapped on it. After a minute or two the upstairs window opened.

'I got the key up here, Missis. I'll drop 'un down.'

It fell with a clink on the stone path. Joanna felt around.

'Got it.'

They let themselves in and found a light switch. Joanna's heart was pounding.

'Mr Bone?'

He was in the front bedroom. He looked at them over the bedclothes, his white head small and tousled above thick vest and striped pyjamas.

'Sorry, Missis.' He was shaken by coughing.

'It's all right, Mr Bone.' Hilary went across to him. 'What is it? I can see you're not well.'

'I got –' His eyes flicked over to Joanna, hovering in the doorway. 'You know, 'tis –'

'Jo,' said Hilary. 'Could you make us all some tea? You don't mind, do you, Mr Bone?'

A few minutes later, she came and put her head into the kitchen.

'I'm going next door to ring his doctor. There's no phone here.'

By the time she came back, the tea was ready.

'Golly, Jo.' Hilary glanced round the kitchen and shivered. 'This kitchen. It can't have changed much in the last eighty years.'

'I know. There's only one cold tap. You have to heat

everything up on that old gas stove. I hadn't a clue how to light it, and the kettle was dreadfully heavy . . .'

'You've done miracles. Do you know –' she closed the door behind her and lowered her voice – 'there's no bathroom here at all. There's only a loo outside in the garden.'

'With violets round the door,' said Joanna.

'Anyway, that's how it all happened. He got up to go and he trod on his catheter –'

'His what?'

It was the doctor who finally explained. She arrived as they were carrying the tea upstairs and they waited downstairs while she examined Mr Bone. Then they all three sat down to a fresh cup of tea at the kitchen table.

'I know,' the doctor said, 'he shouldn't live here alone, especially with a chest like his. But he's very stubborn. He won't move out, won't cut down the cigarettes . . .' She sighed. 'There's a limit to what we can do. It's his choice.'

'But look where it's got him,' Hilary said. 'Alone, frightened, sick . . .'

'And not eating properly,' put in Joanna. 'I saw what he'd had for Sunday lunch, and it was only cheese sandwiches.'

'Yes, well, he won't be alone much longer,' said the doctor. 'I'm getting him into hospital in the morning. His lungs need looking at and I think he's going to need a prostate operation.'

It seemed Mr Bone had had trouble with his bladder for a long time. A drainage tube – a catheter – had been inserted, but he'd stumbled when he'd got up that night and dislodged it, causing himself a lot of pain.

'I've put it right.' The doctor opened the front door. 'He'll sleep now, and the ambulance will be here first thing in the morning. There's nothing more you can do.'

'Thanks for coming so quickly.' Hilary laughed wryly. 'It was a bit outside my normal line of work . . .'

Joanna slipped away and up the stairs. She tapped on the bedroom door.

'Mr Bone?' He was lying flat now. His eyes turned to her enquiringly.

'Can I do anything? Who's going to look after your house while you're in hospital?'

He stirred. 'I in't going to no hospital.'

'Mr Bone —' Joanna came nearer the bed. 'You'll have to. They'll make you feel much better.'

His eyelids were drooping. 'My house don't need no looking after. I'll be home in a day or two. There's just Billy . . .'

'Billy? Oh, your budgie. I'll look after him, Mr Bone. He can come in next door with us.'

'Seed,' he said. 'Downstairs.' He was asleep.

She collected the cage and found the birdseed. Then she and Hilary went outside, across to their own front door and back to bed.

Morning came all too quickly.

Joanna got ready for school, her mind still muzzy from the broken night. She kept looking out of the window for Mr Bone's ambulance.

'He'll be much better in hospital,' said Hilary, doing her eye make-up. 'He can't expect to go on for ever in the old way. The doctor says he's got no family. He needs to be sensible . . .'

'Yes,' said Joanna. She was topping up Billy's seed container. 'Only —'

'Look, the ambulance,' Hilary interrupted. 'I'll just pop next door and see if they need a hand. And I'll tell Mr Bone we'll look after his greenhouse plants and things. Then we must go. See you down by the car.'

'OK.'

Joanna collected her bag and wandered out of the house. The ambulance was waiting at Mr Bone's gate, its doors ready open. A haze of bluebells lay under the hedge; somewhere in the distance a cuckoo was calling.

She stood still.

So that was what he'd been doing last evening.

Monday was rubbish collection day. Their own full black plastic sack stood in the lane, ready to be picked up when the dustcart came along. Mr Bone had put a sack out too. But that wasn't all that stood by his gate. Joanna went closer to look.

There were cardboard boxes, piled one upon another, and bulging brown paper bags. Perhaps a fox had pawed at them in the night, because their contents had spilled out into the lane. She saw shoes and necklaces, brooches and blouses; a pair of kid gloves, some blue knitting wool, a hair brush . . .

He must have taken it all from his loft last night and dumped it out here. He hadn't bothered to stack any of it neatly, or protect it from foxes, because everything here was destined for the rubbish tip and the incinerator.

She stooped and picked up a photograph, and wiped the mud off it with her finger. She found herself looking down at a little dark-haired girl. The photograph was small, just a head and shoulders portrait, oval-shaped.

Jessie Bone.

Joanna gave a quick glance round. Then she dropped the photograph into her school bag and began rummaging in the top carton.

Her fingers closed round something hard and she drew it out. It was a thick notebook with silky dark green covers.

She flipped through it. It was full of writing, page after page after page. The ink was faded and brown, the handwriting old-fashioned and hard to read.

A diary?

She looked again, puzzled.

More like letters. Dozens and dozens of letters.

She turned back to the first page of the book and read:

I feel so happy tonight I got to tell somebody. But who? Not Harold, that's for certain, or Leonard, and Frank would probably laugh. And Minna's my friend but she don't understand – not this, she don't.

Then suddenly I thought – tell Alice.

When I was small – really small – I used to come running to you, all upset about something. And you'd say, 'Tell Alice', and you'd put your arm round me and listen, and everything would be all right again.

I'm not miserable this time. I'm happy. So happy, Alice, I must tell you. I left school today and . . .

Alice? Were these letters written to Alice?

She looked at the top of the page. The letter began *Dearest Alice* . . . and it was dated 20th July 1924.

But Alice Bone had died in 1918. Six years earlier.

She looked through the notebook again. Every letter began *Dearest Alice*.

And ended *Your loving sister Jessie*.

There was no more time. Joanna heard voices and looked up to see two ambulancemen carrying Mr Bone out of his house, trussed up in red blankets. She pushed the notebook into her bag and hurriedly went to stand by the car.

'Morning.' The men smiled at her as they passed. 'The lady's just tidying up. She says she'll be out in a minute.'

Mr Bone's eyes were closed. She watched as he was loaded in, and the doors shut. Then the ambulance bumped away down the lane.

Almost before it was out of sight she heard the dustcart coming from the other direction. She pressed close to the car as the vehicle jolted into view, snorting and roaring.

Two men in orange jackets jumped down. They picked up the black sacks and tossed them into the back of the vehicle. The cartons and the bags followed, and all the bits and pieces strewn by Mr Bone's gate. Giant steel jaws clamped down on to them, chewed into them, and they were ground and mashed up with all the rest of the rubbish.

Within a minute, the monster had gone.

Quiet descended on Violet Bottom once more.

Chapter Nine

Joanna climbed into the school bus.

'Come and sit in the back, Jo-Jo.'

'Come on, Jo-Jo. Give yourself a treat.'

There was an empty seat next to Richard at the front. She hesitated, but he didn't look up and the headphones were in his ears as usual. She went past him and found a seat halfway back, alone.

The bus left the village and gathered speed. The sky was misty-blue, the fields golden with buttercups.

A notebook and one small photograph. That was all. Everything else of Jessie Bone had gone.

She took out the green notebook and opened it at the first page. And all the shouting and disorder from the back seat dropped away as she began to read:

> . . . I'm not miserable this time. I'm happy. So happy, Alice, I must tell you.
>
> I left school today and it were all right. All year I been dreading it. Not like Minna. She's been counting the days till she could leave. But me, every day as I walked along the lane to school with Minna and Leonard, I'd be thinking, 'Fourteen soon, and no more school. Then what?'
>
> And today the day came. It was our end of term prizegiving and concert.
>
> Miss Bradford said we was all to wear our best. Father came and lots of other people. Father wore his suit . . .

The voices from the back seat of the bus were as noisy and raucous as ever. But as Joanna read on, they faded away.

She was no longer on a school bus. She was with Jessie in that village schoolroom in the summer of 1924, listening to George Bone and the headmistress, Miss Bradford, as they talk:

'Yes, I'll be keeping Jessie at home, at least for a year or two.'

He stands easily among the desks and slates of the schoolroom, his boots polished to a deep shine, his hat in his hands.

'To my mind, a young maid like Jessie's best off at home. Anyhow, we couldn't none of us spare her, could we, Jessie?' He smiles down at his daughter, and her heart gives a twist. 'She's taken care of us ever since my older daughter Alice passed to her rest.'

'Yes, indeed, Mr Bone. You must be proud of her. And we shall miss her here.'

Miss Bradford doesn't like Jessie. Jessie knows that. Once, in singing class, she'd said, 'Now, who shall I ask to sing a solo?' and Jessie had put up her hand.

'Ah, the cocky little Bone girl,' Miss Bradford had exclaimed and, after that, she never chose Jessie to sing if she could help it. 'Too cocky by half, Jessie,' she'd say.

But today she says, 'Her work has been first class, Mr Bone. Her sewing is especially pleasing.'

He nods. 'She'll be keeping on with the sewing. My neighbour, Mrs Kellaway, has fixed Jessie up with a nice little job to do at home. She can earn herself a bit of money and learn something about dressmaking at the same time. It's never too early to start learning a trade.'

'Oh, certainly,' Miss Bradford says. 'Excuse me, Mr Bone.' The gentry are arriving in their motor cars.

Mr Tom Mahler, the young assistant teacher who has recently come to the school from the north of England, moves to his place at the piano. He smiles at Jessie.

Everybody makes speeches: the Rector, Miss Bradford,

Sir Wilfred. It's very warm. Jessie watches Mrs Kellaway's head drooping and jerking up again, and Miss Pamela, up on the platform with her parents, fiddling with her white gloves and staring all around.

Then the school-leavers are called up. Lady Emily gives them each a book. Jessie's book is *Lamb's Tales from Shakespeare*. There is a second book, as the sewing prize. She sees Minna clapping as hard as she can and wishes the prize could have gone to Minna instead.

Lady Emily shakes her hand and keeps hold of it.

'Bone's little girl,' she says. 'Our stone mason, Bone.'

'Yes, my lady.'

She nods to herself. 'I remember. From Violet Bottom.'

'Yes, my lady.' There is a queue behind Jessie and the applause has stopped.

'You sing. I hear you sing at concerts. Are you singing today for us?'

Jessie's face is hot. Miss Bradford's frowning at her.

'Yes, my lady.'

'Excellent,' says Lady Emily and pats her hand. 'Excellent.'

Then the concert begins. And, at the end, Jessie sings.

She sings 'Early One Morning' and 'Greensleeves' and her clear, pure soprano effortlessly reaches into every dusty corner of the old schoolroom. At the end, she sings 'There Is a Land of Pure Delight'. And as she sings it, she thinks of Alice:

> There everlasting spring abides,
> And never-withering flowers:
> Death, like a narrow sea, divides
> That heavenly land from ours.

She pictures Alice, safe in that land. Alice used to tell Jessie she would become a famous singer if she worked hard enough, and Father has told her she must be the mother to the family. Jessie thinks how, one day, when she reaches the Land of Pure Delight herself, she'll be able to tell Alice that she has done it all.

And, as she and her father leave the schoolroom to go home to Violet Bottom, something wonderful happens.

Lady Emily stops them and says, 'A remarkable voice, Bone. That voice must be cherished.'

George Bone gives his rare smile, full of pride.

'Jessie sings very nicely, my lady. At church concerts . . .'

'Cherished.' Sir Wilfred is signalling from the door, but Lady Emily ignores him. 'She has a power to move one to tears.'

Jessie looks at Lady Emily and sees it is true. She has been crying.

'Mr Mahler.'

'Yes?' Some people in the village say Mr Mahler has dangerously socialist views. He speaks to Lady Emily just as he speaks to everyone else.

Lady Emily talks to him about Jessie's voice, about finding her a singing teacher who will help her. Jessie waits, hardly breathing, holding tightly to her father's arm.

At last Lady Emily turns back.

'There is a teacher in Dorchester. A Mr Cadwallader. Mr Mahler will let you know, Bone, when the lessons will commence. Good day.'

She moves on.

'Oh, Father . . .'

'One moment, Jessie. My lady . . .'

Lady Emily tilts her head. 'I am sure Sir Wilfred would adjust your wages a little, Bone, if the cost . . .'

Father stiffens. 'No need for that, my lady. Jessie will be earning from her sewing work. My children have been brought up to understand that pleasures must be paid for. I just want Jessie to say thank you, my lady . . .'

* * *

61

That is what happened, Alice.

This morning, I had nothing to look forward to but doing the housework and sewing with Mrs Kellaway. And now I'm going to become a great singer. You used to say I would but, Alice, I knew it already, even before you taught me the notes on the piano. I've felt it inside me. Like a bird fluttering in a cage, wanting to get out.

I must stop in a minute. There are seven shirts waiting to be ironed. I'll write again soon.

Mr Mahler give me this beautiful notebook today as a leaving present. He said he knew I would have a lot to write in it one day.

And I will. I won't let him down. Or you, I promise. I'll do my best to look after Father and the boys as you did, and I'll work and work at singing.

Oh, Alice, there's so much I want to do. Isn't it wonderful?

Your loving sister

Je –

The notebook was snatched from Joanna's hand.

'Hey! Give that back!'

'Don't get your knickers in a twist, I only want to look.' Vivien held the notebook out of reach. 'What's this then? The Secret Diary of Jo-Jo, aged 14¾?'

'You've got no right –' Joanna made a grab for it. There were screams of laughter from the back seat.

'Go on, Viv. Give us a squint at it.'

'Don't –'

'Chuck it over here.'

'Don't you DARE –'

The driver turned round. 'Cut that out, you lot.'

'Oooh.' They pretended to shiver in fear.

Joanna grabbed again and managed to seize the notebook. She thrust it into her bag, panting.

'You're just so – so babyish. So stupid. Can't you grow up?'

'No, they can't.'

Joanna turned round. Richard was standing in the aisle, white-knuckled as he held on to the backs of the seats, his headphones slung round his neck, the music faintly buzzing and beating into the air. 'They're just not capable of it.'

There was a roar of delight from the back seat.

'Not capable!'

'You should know, Richie.'

'Ask Viv if Richie's capable. Go on, Viv, tell us –'

Richard's face flamed. Without another word, he turned and went back to his seat. Vivien's crowd cheered and stamped their feet. Joanna saw Richard push the headphones back in his ears.

She spent the last five minutes of the journey staring out of the window. She found she was shaking.

Why should I put up with this? she thought. It's so . . . stupid. Better to be Jessie, leaving school at fourteen and getting free of it all.

I'll tell you one thing, she said to herself. I'm never travelling on this bus again.

Chapter Ten

It was the lunch hour. Joanna was sitting on a bench in a sunny corner outside the physics lab.

'Hi, Joanna.'

She looked up. It was Becky and her friend Leela.

'Mind if we sit down?'

'No. Help yourself.'

They sat on the bench. Becky grinned at her.

'Not interrupting you, are we? We'll go away if we are.'

'You're not.' Suddenly she was glad to see them.

'Only, we thought,' Becky said. 'You know . . .'

'We thought you looked lonely,' Leela spoke more directly. 'And we thought you might like some company. You seem to be on your own all the time.'

'Not all the time,' said Joanna. 'I'm on the bus twice a day.'

'Ah,' said Becky. 'The bus. With Vivien Dennis and her lot. Mrs Greenhill's brilliant idea that Vivien would look after you. How's it going?'

Joanna thought for a minute. 'Fine,' she said.

They looked at her. Becky's dark eyebrows went up. Leela was beginning to smile.

'Truly?'

'Honestly?'

'No,' said Joanna. 'It's awful. Absolutely, a hundred per cent awful. I hate it.'

'Yes,' said Becky. 'We thought you might. You look the sort of person who would.'

Something in Joanna glowed warm, recognised as a person who didn't belong with Vivien's crowd.

'If you hate the bus as much as all that,' Becky was saying, 'why travel with them? You don't have to.'

'I know what they're like,' Leela put in. 'They pick on anyone new. Different. Before you it was me.'

'Was it?'

'Oh, yes. I'm the only person in our year who isn't white, in case you hadn't noticed. I made a nice change for them. They're so –' She gestured in the air, fastidiously.

'Yes.'

Becky said, 'And there's always Richard, of course. Poor old Richard.'

'Why doesn't he stand up for himself?' Joanna asked. 'Why don't you?'

Joanna opened her mouth, and shut it again. 'I'm new,' she said at last. 'I will one day. I tried this morning . . .'

'What happened?'

'They laughed.' She caught Becky's eye. 'Oh, OK. It's not that easy, I admit. But it could be done.'

'Not if you're as stuck on Vivien as Richard is.'

They laughed at her stunned face. 'True,' said Leela. 'He worships her. Vivien even let him take her to the cinema last term. He's never got over it.'

'Anyway,' Becky said. 'If you don't want to travel with them, Joanna, I wouldn't.'

Billy didn't seem to be a budgerigar who talked. Joanna tried him with a few obvious phrases like, 'Hello, Billy,' and 'Who's a pretty boy, then?' but Billy just rubbed his beak backwards and forwards against the bars and looked at her with one bright eye.

'Mum?'

Hilary was shredding lettuce in the kitchen.

'Yes? Slice those tomatoes, will you?'

'Mum,' Joanna picked up a tomato, 'I think I'll cycle to school from now on.'

She'd thought about it all the way home in the bus that afternoon. Why shouldn't she cycle? She'd brought her bicycle down from London, picturing herself riding round the Dorset countryside. She hadn't actually used it yet. Now was the opportunity.

'Jo, it's too far,' Hilary said. 'Isn't it?'

'Only eight or nine miles. No problem.'

'But you'll be on your own if you cycle. I thought you were enjoying it on the bus, all travelling together.'

'Not particularly.' Joanna arranged her tomato slices carefully on a plate.

'Oh.' Hilary bit her lip. 'I'm sorry. I thought – you know – they'd be nice country children.'

'In sunbonnets and smocks? Too much Thomas Hardy, Mum. I don't suppose they're any different from London kids, really.'

Of course they weren't. They just seemed worse because, for the first time in her life, she was facing everything alone.

'Well, I suppose you could try cycling for a week or two,' Hilary said, doubtfully. 'But you're to wear a helmet, mind. If you'd seen half the injuries I've seen at work . . . Just be careful, Jo. Be very careful, won't you?'

They were working in the garden after tea when the phone rang. Hilary went to answer it. Joanna continued pulling up weeds around the strawberry plants. The plants were in flower now, and she could see the pale fruit beginning to form.

'Jo . . .' Hilary was beckoning from the open window. Joanna went across.

'It's Dad.' She smiled at her. 'For you.'

'What does he want?'

'Just keeping in touch. Like we agreed. Come on, darling.'

Slowly, Joanna went into the house, wiped her hands and picked up the phone.

'Hello.'

'How are you, Jo?'

'I'm OK,' Joanna said. 'Thank you. How are you?'

He laughed. 'You sound very polite.'

'No point in being anything else.' Joanna rubbed her arm. Something had bitten her out in the garden.

'Mum tells me it's all going well down there. Sounds like fun.'

She didn't answer. Billy was hopping from perch to perch. She pictured Corinne lolling on a sofa just behind her father, smiling as she listened.

'Jo . . .' Her father cleared his throat.

'Yes?'

'Nothing. Nothing really. As long as you're all right.'

'We're coping,' she said. 'Nothing for you to worry about.'

'That's good.'

There was another silence.

'Patrick sends his love,' he said at last.

'Thanks.'

'Jo, I'm putting a cheque in the post for you. Buy yourself . . .'

'No,' she said. 'I don't want any money. I told you, we're coping. Look, I've got to go now.'

'Me too. Time to cook supper.'

'Oh.' Clearly, Corinne wasn't the cooking type.

''Bye, then, Jo. Take care, darling. I'll ring again soon.'

'Goodbye,' she said and put the phone down.

That night, Joanna sat up in bed, staring at the face in the little oval photograph. A little girl's face, perhaps seven years old, dark hair tied with a big white ribbon. Jessie Bone's photograph. Probably taken just a short time before her sister Alice died.

Joanna propped the picture up against her bedside radio and flicked the radio on, low so as not to disturb her mother in the next bedroom. She needed to cover up the silence from the empty cottage next door.

What was Mr Bone feeling at this moment, lying in a hospital bed? For all she knew, this might be the first night he'd ever spent away from Violet Bottom.

She reached out for Jessie's green notebook, then stopped, seeing again the sacks and bags waiting for the dustcart. The old man had tried to send everything to do with Jessie to the incinerator. What right had she to interfere, to probe into the secrets of the Bone family?

But –

Her mind began to argue back. He made his choice; he put the notebook out with the rubbish. But it's not rubbish to me. It's interesting. Jessie lived just the other side of that wall. I've got a right to look at it. I rescued it.

Stole it, you mean.

He was ill, she said to herself; old and ill. He didn't know what he was doing. One day, I'll give the notebook and the photograph back to him and he'll be pleased. Meanwhile . . .

1st August 1924

Dearest Alice,

Friday evenings are special.

For years, ever since I was eight, I've sat at the supper table with Harold and Frank and Leonard, with the housekeeping purse and the account book open in front of me, ready for Father to check. When I started I just couldn't get it to add up properly, there were so many things to remember and write in. The groceries, and shoe mending, and a new saucepan or the knives sharpened . . . Oh, everything. Mrs Kellaway used to try and help me get it straight before Father saw it, but even then he'd often find it a penny or two out.

Of course I got used to it. I'd made up my mind I'd be as good at running the house as you'd been, Alice.

And tonight – well – tonight was different. For the first time, I had some wages too . . .

Joanna's eyelids were beginning to droop. She put out a hand and switched the radio off, and went on drowsily reading.

The lamp throws a golden light on the supper table, and on to the circle of hands lying on the cloth.

George Bone's hands, scrubbed clean of stone dust, reckon up the column of figures in the account book, then slit open his wage packet, spilling out banknotes and coins. Most of it is passed over to his daughter, a ten-shilling note kept for himself.

Harold's fingers, thin and irritable, push his clerk's wage packet across to his father. Three silver halfcrowns come back to him for his night-school classes and bus fares.

Frank's hands, large, weather-tanned, slump in apology. This week there's only seven-and-sixpence, just a little job he helped a friend with. But he's heard of a farmer who's looking for some help. By next Friday he's sure . . .

Leonard, at eleven years old, has hands that are still a child's. But he produces three shillings he's made from selling eggs and vegetables. Two copper threepenny bits come spinning back to him and he tucks them away in his pocket.

Lastly, Jessie's hands, moving with their usual assurance to collect the money her father passes to her, and put it into the old leather purse. The hands are rough and discoloured from scrubbing soap and washing soda, the fingertips sore and scratched from a week of pushing a needle through heavy material but, as she opens her own wage packet for the first time and displays the fifteen shillings inside, they tremble a little from excitement.

Ten shillings for the purse, to help feed and clothe the

family. The rest – five shillings – is set carefully on one side.

'All of it?' questions her father. 'All of it for those lessons of yours?'

Jessie glances at the photograph on the wall of Alice, gently smiling.

'Yes, Father. All of it.'

Jessie Bone, at fourteen, has left childhood behind.

Chapter Eleven

The dry, sunny days of May gave way to June and, overnight, the weather changed. The wind swung round to the west, and day after day dark rain clouds swept in low over the Dorset hills. The sea off the Weymouth coast was blotted out in wet mist, and raindrops dripped from the statue of Thomas Hardy as he sat gazing at the swirling traffic of Dorchester. Each morning cars and motor cycles were joined by huge continental lorries heading for the French ports of Cherbourg or Caen, and they all splashed along the winding roads in a whirl of spray and exhaust fumes.

In the midst of it, Joanna battled on.

As she left Violet Bottom each morning for school, enormous puddles lay in the lane and her cycle wheels sank in the soft mud; on the main roads, she was forced close into the hedgerows as cars and trucks swished past. By the time she lifted her head and wiped the rain from her face and saw at last the school in the distance, her legs were aching and she was often soaked right through.

But it was worth it. It was worth it on the occasional mornings when the sun broke through the clouds and gleamed on the wet road under her tyres; when she saw a pheasant or a baby rabbit scuttling for cover under a hedge, or a group of silver-winged gulls wheel above a field of green wheat. Above all, it was worth it every morning when the school bus overtook her near the school gates, and a row of laughing figures turned round to point at her from the back seat.

Everything was worth it then. She was doing things her way. She was free.

*   *   *

But not everyone saw it like that.

One afternoon at school they were putting finishing touches to the exhibition about the Lansbury Abbas area in the twentieth century.

'Hold that picture still, you two,' Vivien called, stepping back a pace. 'No, it's miles out.'

Joanna, balanced on a stepladder, sighed and tilted her end of the huge photograph slightly.

'For goodness sake, Jo-Jo. Not you. Him. Beanpole.'

Richard's ears reddened. They adjusted the picture until at last even Vivien was satisfied and it was safely fastened to the wall.

Joanna climbed down and stood back to study the grainy, black and white photograph properly. It showed two parlourmaids in ankle-length dresses, white caps and frilled pinafores carrying tea out on to the lawns of Ennington Hall. In the shade of a cedar tree Sir Wilfred, Lady Emily and their guests waited at a table to receive it.

A matching picture, already in place on the wall, showed the same cedar tree. But this picture had been taken about seventy years later, after the estate had become a country park. Little clusters of people in T-shirts, jeans or shorts sprawled on the lawns now, licking ice creams, drinking from cans or simply sunbathing.

'That's OK.' She started to fold up the stepladder. Silently, Richard came over to help.

'Thanks.'

He nodded. Then he said, 'You've given up the bus.'

'Yes. I –' Why should she explain? 'I'd rather cycle.'

'Oh.' He leaned the ladder against the wall. 'You like cycling, do you?'

She glanced out of the window. It was just starting to rain again.

'Not specially. But I've got a right . . .'

The bell for the end of school broke into what she was saying.

'What?'

'I've got a right to go to school,' she repeated, 'without putting up with all that stuff, you know what I mean. I hate it. Why should I put up with it? I'd rather get soaked every day.'

'So you're getting soaked . . .' He was frowning to himself, as if working out a difficult calculation, '. . . and they're staying dry. You're letting them win, aren't you?'

'No,' Joanna said. 'I'm winning.'

People were making for the door now. Richard picked up his bag, and took out his personal stereo.

'You shouldn't let them get to you,' he said. 'I don't. I just listen to my music and totally ignore them.'

Joanna was left standing in the hall.

Rubbish, she thought. Richard goes on the bus because he can't bear not to see Vivien. And they do get to him sometimes. I've seen it happen. He ought to admit it. It's all just one big cover-up.

Chapter Twelve

The history exhibition opened the next day. Classes of children from other schools were brought in to see displays, to hear talks and watch videos. Then, in the evening, it was the turn of the parents and members of the public.

'Hello, Mum.' Joanna caught sight of Hilary through the crowd. 'OK?'

Hilary smiled and nodded and vanished again.

The corner where Joanna stood with Richard and Vivien was devoted to the subject of IN SERVICE AT THE BIG HOUSE. As well as photographs and newspapers there were displays of household equipment that servants would have used: flat irons, carpet sweepers, Monkey Brand soap. And the interview with Minna Kellaway had been turned into a booklet, with pictures of her as a young housemaid in her new uniform, and as the old lady she now was.

'Is she here?' asked Richard. 'I haven't seen her yet.'

'Over there.' Joanna pointed. 'Coming in now with that fat man.'

'That's my father,' said Vivien. 'He drove her here.'

'Oh. Sorry.'

Vivien shrugged, and began tidying the already tidy booklets.

'Hello, Viv. How are you doing, Richard?'

Miss Kellaway leaned on her walking frame, seeming smaller than ever by the side of the Rector's bulk, and looked at the booklets fanned out on the table, each bearing her face on the cover.

'Fancy,' she said.

Mr Dennis stretched out his hand to Joanna across the

table. 'Don't think we've met, have we? Introduce us, Viv.'

'Jo- Joanna Milford,' Vivien muttered. 'My father.'

'She lives in my old house, Rector,' said Miss Kellaway. 'Down in Violet Bottom.'

She seemed friendlier tonight, as if she'd forgotten they hadn't parted on very good terms after the interview. 'Oh, look at them old carpet sweepers. Never expected to see them on show. Mind you, we thought they were wonderful when we first got them. We just had brooms before that, with tea leaves to keep down the dust.'

Later, when things weren't so busy, Joanna caught up with Miss Kellaway again looking at Becky and Leela's display of twentieth-century fashions. There was an outfit for each decade of the century, from the heavy skirts and high-necked blouses of Edwardian days to the flimsy clothes of the present. Joanna pointed to a short, tube-like dress of the 1920s, covered in glittering beads.

'Did you ever wear anything like that?'

'No, no. My mother wouldn't have let me. They was for the gentry, for their dances and suchlike.'

'People must have been a totally different shape in those days.' Becky looked down at herself ruefully. 'I'd never squeeze into that dress.'

'Sometimes the young ladies like Miss Pamela –' Miss Kellaway smiled to herself – 'used to bind themselves round the chest to make themselves flat enough.'

'Ugh . . .'

'All these beads.' Leela fingered the dress. 'I suppose someone sat sewing them all on by hand. Who'd ever have the patience now?'

Miss Kellaway had moved on, staring at a picture of Sir Wilfred and some friends shooting on the estate. Joanna hurried after her.

'Miss Kellaway, did Jessie Bone do that sort of thing?'

The old lady turned round sharply. 'What sort of thing?'

'Sewing beads on dresses. For the gentry.'

Miss Kellaway's mouth tightened.

'Sometimes she did. Once they come into fashion. But I don't want to talk about Jessie Bone. T'wouldn't be right.'

'You were her friend, Miss Kellaway.' Joanna looked at her with exasperation. 'Why won't you tell me about her? Mr Bone said –'

'Leonard? What did he say?'

Joanna hesitated, looking into the bright-eyed, anxious gaze. She'd been going to say *Mr Bone said the same as you. That he wouldn't talk about her.* But if she told Miss Kellaway that, she'd never learn anything.

She picked her words carefully. 'Mr Bone said Jessie was his older sister. I asked him all about her. He had a photograph of her. And some letters.'

She saw the mouth relax. 'Oh, if he's shown you things like that . . .'

Joanna nodded encouragingly. She reached out for a chair and helped the old lady to sit down.

'I hadn't seen no picture of Jess for years, till you showed me that carnival one so sudden, dear. It give me quite a turn.'

'Yes, I see.'

'We used to have such fun, me and Jess.' Her eyes were distant now, remembering. 'We was just the same age, see. And after Alice passed away, we was the only girls down there at Violet Bottom. Jess had a houseful of men. Her dad . . . three brothers . . .'

'Harold and Frank,' said Joanna. 'And Leonard. What were they like?'

Miss Kellaway pursed her lips.

'Well . . . Harold I never cared for over much. Jess didn't neither, perhaps.' She shook her head. 'Looked just like his dad, tall and thin, always knew what other folk should be doing. But he were a cold fish, Harold, and his dad were never that.'

'What about Frank?'

She shook her head again, but smiling this time.

'That's Frank, up there.'

'Where?' Joanna swivelled round. 'Oh, that shooting picture.'

'On the left there. Frank and his pals used to go beating for the gentry. Walking in front of them, slashing at the undergrowth, making the birds fly up for the guns. They'd earn a bit of money . . . When they wasn't out poaching the birds themselves, that is. Oh, Frank were a bad lad sometimes.'

Joanna looked at the young man on the edge of the group, round-faced and grinning under his flat cap.

'He looks fun. And Leonard?'

'Oh, Leonard you knows already. He don't never change. Just the same now as when he were a little kiddy – keeping himself to himself, not saying much. You never really knew what he were thinking. Bit like –'

She stopped.

'Like who, Miss Kellaway?' Joanna asked softly. 'Like Jessie?'

She moved uneasily, her pale blue eyes distressed. 'Jess got hurt by things. Hurt bad. And didn't show it.'

'What things?'

'Well . . .' Miss Kellaway considered. 'She had this job, same as my mother, doing sewing at home for a dressmaker called Miss Mountain. Miss Mountain'd bring the stuff over from Dorchester once a week, and Mother and Jess would sit in our front room and sew. That's what her dad wanted, so she could be on the spot to look after the house, get the meals and so on. And Jess'd do anything to please her dad. But . . .'

'But what?'

'Jess had her singing, you see. Always her singing . . .'

From the corner of her eye, Joanna saw the Rector heading towards them, carrying a tea tray, followed by Mr Rawlinson and the deputy head. She said urgently, 'Miss

Kellaway, just one more thing. Please. Where's Jessie now?' If she was dead, wouldn't her name be on the family headstone in the churchyard?

'Excuse me, Joanna.' The Rector set down the tray. 'Now, Miss Kellaway, we want to introduce you to everyone. We can't have the star of the evening hiding in a corner, can we?'

Joanna escaped.

At the end of the evening, when she and her mother walked through the school car park, there was only a faint glow of sunset left in the western sky.

They were tying Joanna's bicycle on to the roof rack of the Fiat when the Rector and Vivien came past.

'All right, Joanna?' he asked, stopping to give a hand. 'How enterprising of you to cycle to school. Why have you never done that, Viv?'

'I'm too lazy, Dad.' It was the other Vivien again, Joanna thought cynically. The one who'd been so sweet in her little pink frock.

'I'm not very happy about it, actually,' Hilary said. 'The traffic's so heavy. But Jo didn't seem to like the bus.'

Mr Dennis raised his shaggy eyebrows. 'Really? Viv's always been happy with it.'

The two girls stood about awkwardly, not looking at each other. Hilary and the Rector began talking about Violet Bottom.

'Yes, you must find it isolated after London, especially now Leonard Bone's not there. Poor old chap. I popped in to the hospital to see him the other day.'

'How was he?' asked Joanna.

The Rector shook his head. 'I don't think he'll be back to live on his own. He's going to have to accept that.' He sighed. 'What a business old age is. Which reminds me – Miss Kellaway's sitting inside waiting for us to bring the car round. Come on, Viv.'

'Goodnight, Mrs Milford,' Vivien called.

'Nice girl,' said Hilary. 'Perhaps she'll cycle with you sometimes. It'd make me feel better if there were two of you.'

'Mum, for goodness sake . . .'

In the car Joanna sat silent, looking out into the dark night. If Leonard Bone was really not coming home again, then Jessie's diaries were as good as hers. Why have any scruples about reading them? Sometimes she got tired of thinking about that sort of thing.

'I wonder if there's a youth club in the village,' Hilary said, changing down on a long hill. 'It'd be nice for you to get out in the evenings, wouldn't it? I should have asked the Rector. Oh, by the way –'

'What?' The roads were almost empty, the car eating up the miles. It was all so easy compared with cycling.

'Dad phoned, just as I was leaving this evening. Wanted to talk to you.'

Joanna glanced up. 'What about?'

'Your birthday.' She smiled. 'He seems to have ideas about it.'

'Ideas? You discussed it all, did you? Cooked something up between you?'

There was a small silence.

'Jo, don't be silly. We don't cook things up between us.'

'Sounds like it. I'm sick of people organising my whole life, telling me to join youth clubs, organising my birthday. I'm nearly fifteen, I can make decisions, you know.'

'OK,' said Hilary, sounding surprised. 'Calm down.'

Before Jessie was my age, Joanne thought, she was earning her own living, running a house, training as a singer . . . Jessie's father treated her like an adult. My father cooks up little birthday treats and sends me those wretched cheques, as if I was a child. He's like a child himself.

Pictures came into her mind of Dad at school functions in the old days. Dad belonged to a jazz band, and once or twice he brought the band to play at school fêtes and things, a little group of middle-aged men dressed up in striped waistcoats and bowler hats, blowing instruments. Joanna remembered them playing to the crowds, everybody laughing and clapping. Meanwhile her mother washed up in a hot kitchen, or stood behind a stall for hours and hours. Or Dad would wander in towards the end of an afternoon, when nearly all the work had been done, stand on a soapbox and run an auction of all the unsold goods. People loved that. Joanna probably even loved it herself when she was younger. But not now. Now she could see Dad had never really grown up.

'Mum, it's *my* birthday. There's no need for you two to discuss it when I'm not even there.'

Hilary gave a sigh.

'Look, it's late, Jo. We're both tired. Dad's going to ring again tomorrow. Let's leave it all till then, can we?'

Chapter Thirteen

'Hello, Jo. It's Dad.'

'Yes.'

'How are you, darling?'

'All right, thank you.'

'That's good. Jo, about your birthday.'

'What about it?' Joanna picked up Billy's millet spray which had fallen on to the table, and pushed it back between the bars.

'Well, you're not fifteen every day. We – Patrick and I – thought, seeing your birthday's on a Saturday, you might like to have a change from all that country air and come up to Town for the weekend.'

Silence.

'Jo? We could go to a couple of shows, or on the river or something. Like we did when you were small. Remember?'

'No, not really.'

'Oh. Well, we can do whatever you like. And there's plenty of room here, darling, for you to stay.'

'What –' Joanna cleared her throat.

'Sorry?'

'What about Mum?'

Silence his end this time.

'I'm sure Mum would spare you for the weekend. We've just been talking about it.'

'I'd rather stay here.'

'Oh. Of course, if you've got something exciting lined up for your birthday . . .'

'Yes.' Billy was chirruping to his reflection in his mirror.

'Well, fair enough. I only –'

'I've got to go now.'

'All right, darling. 'Bye now. Take care.'

'Goodbye.' She laid the receiver down.

'Sorry,' she added.

The next evening, Joanna sat alone in the living room at Violet Bottom.

It was over an hour since Hilary had gone out, saying that it was a lovely evening for once and she felt like a walk.

'You'll be all right here for a bit, won't you, Jo? I expect you've still got some homework to do.'

'I've finished.' She didn't much like the idea of being there alone, despite the evening sun. 'I'll come with you, shall I?'

'I'd rather go on my own.'

'Oh.'

Left alone, Joanna flicked through the TV channels, switched off again, made herself a sandwich, wandered round the cottage. It still seemed terribly cramped compared with the house in London; there were boxfuls of possessions stacked in the tiny hall because there seemed nowhere else to put them.

Finally she settled herself in a patch of evening sun by the window. This was where Mrs Kellaway and Jessie had once sat, sewing.

She picked up the green notebook:

9th December 1924

. . . All morning me and Mrs Kellaway sat by the window to catch the light for working, not wanting to light the lamp so early.

We didn't think Minna would get down here for her half day, but she come about three, quite covered with snow. She went off again in half an hour, hoping to get back to the Big House before dark. She brought us some lardy cake . . .

Tonight the lane's all filled up with snow; it looks

quite ghostly outside. I'm praying it'll thaw by tomorrow. I must go to Dorchester for my lesson . . .

10th December 1924
. . . I got there safely, though I thought the men would have to get out and push the bus up the hills. When we arrived I ran through the streets to Mr Cadwallader's, I was so glad to be there . . .

Oh, Alice, Mr Cadwallader's teaching me so much. He tells me about the great singers and what they had to suffer. I'm just beginning to see how much there is to learn . . .

The walls are hung with anatomical drawings of the throat and larynx. Mr Cadwallader asks his wife to open the window wide, and the cold clear air pours into the room.

'Now, Miss Bone,' he says.

She places a hand on her diaphragm and breathes in. After a second or two, she releases it; 'Ah,' she sings softly, and is aware of the control she is beginning to have on her muscles, her breathing, her voice. 'Ah – ah – ah.'

'An open throat, Miss Bone,' says Mr Cadwallader. 'That is what we are working to attain. Our progress must be slow and careful, a step at a time. So, once more, if you please.'

Jessie takes up her position again.

'Breathe, Miss Bone . . . And hold it . . .'

. . . the shop windows was full of Christmas stuff, and chickens and geese hanging up outside the butcher's. I stopped on the way back to the bus to buy Leonard some twists of barley sugar. A band was playing carols at the top of the High Street and I felt very happy . . .

Father overtook me in the lane going home. He'd been working all day on the roof of the Big House, checking for damage. He was frozen to death. I'd banked the fire well up before I left, but it was nearly out. Then there was the supper to cook. Poor Father's hands was numb with cold . . .

10th April 1925
. . . It's Good Friday. A lovely sunny, windy day for me and Father to walk to church. I do love Easter time.

Before the service started we took flowers to the churchyard. It hardly needed no more, Alice, it were so full of primroses already, and the birds nesting in the trees and singing their hearts out . . .

We spent the day quietly at home. Father read to us from the Bible and he asked me to sing an Easter hymn before we went to bed . . .

2nd July 1925
. . . Frank and Cyril Wragge are trying to build a crystal set. They want to listen in to the wireless programmes. They told me to stop playing the piano because they was trying to get a signal on their cat's whisker thing. They swore they had one but I couldn't hear nothing on it, we was laughing so much.

I went out in the garden to pick some beans for supper. Mrs Kellaway give me some strawberries. 'For your dad,' she said. She don't never give up with Father. She'd marry him like a shot if he'd have her . . .

Leonard was fetching water from the well for the garden. At least we've got the pump in the kitchen now, so we don't have to haul the water up all the time like we used to . . .

Joanna looked up from the notebook. It was growing too dark in the room to read Jessie's faded handwriting. She took the notebook outside, and saw the sun was just slipping behind the edge of the hills.

Where was Mum? She didn't usually go out for walks on her own like that. Besides, where was there to walk? The land on both sides of the lane was farm land. Joanna tried to imagine Mum striding across fields of cows and through farmyards full of barking dogs, but she couldn't make the picture work. Mum was such a London person, really.

She went next door and watered the plants in Mr Bone's greenhouse, then went over to the cottage and peered in the dusty window, shielding her eyes with one hand. She could see Alice's photograph on the wall, and Mr Bone's armchair with his newspaper still lying on the seat, a newspaper that would be weeks out of date by now.

Funny to think that old Mr Bone, and Jessie's young brother Leonard hauling buckets of water from the well to the garden, were the same person.

It was a shame the well had been sealed like that; one day she and Mum must get someone to uncover it for them. It would be nice on a hot day to lean over and drop pebbles down and hear them splash in the water.

She went back to her own garden, picked herself a handful of strawberries and sat down on the well cover to go on reading in the last of the evening light:

22nd August 1925

. . . our church outing to Weymouth. Frank and Cyril tried to get me and Minna in the sea, but it was too cold for us.

They all played cricket on the sands and the sun come out for a few minutes. Mrs Kellaway said she were going to have a donkey ride but the man in charge wouldn't let her.

Minna says Harold is sweet on Muriel Parsons. They kept looking at each other over tea, and they sat next to one another on the charabanc home. We had to have the hood up when it started raining. Cyril tried to sit next to me. Minna kept looking at Frank. Is she sweet on him, I wonder?

The men wanted to stop for a drink in Puddletown but the Rector said no. We got back to the village at half-past ten.

Walking home, we met Mr Mahler. He hadn't been on the outing because he don't go to church. He asked me about the singing lessons and I stopped to talk. Then I had to hurry on because the boys was getting impatient. They knew Father would be angry if they left me to walk home in the dark by myself . . .

It might have been rather nice to be looked after as Jessie had been. To have had a father who cared about you as much as Jessie's had, to have been protected everywhere you went.

15th September 1925

. . . Minna was here today, making us laugh. She told us about Miss Pamela's friends from London, six of them in a bright red motor car. Minna saw them out of the window at the Big House when she was making beds. They come driving in through the gates with the horn honking. They nearly overturned Lady Emily going along in her pony and trap.

I put my sewing down while Minna was talking. Mrs Kellaway said, 'Come on now, Jess. Keep sewing or you won't get no money.'

At that, I refused to do another stitch.

'Give it here, Jess,' said Minna. 'Sing to us instead.'

So I sang them my new song. It's by Schubert. The German words are really hard to get just right.

Harold come home in the middle of it. He said I didn't ought to sing German songs, they was unpatriotic.

Such nonsense. Just because his tea weren't ready . . .

25th September 1925

. . . I'm very sleepy, and my bed's made up, but I daren't lie down in case I doze off.

Frank's still not in. He crept out nearly two hours ago, once Father and the other two boys was asleep. He'll tap on the window when he comes back, so I can let him in.

It's lucky for him I sleep down here in the parlour. He knows I wouldn't never tell Father what he's up to.

He and Cyril think I don't know, but I do. They're out on Sir Wilfred's land looking for pheasants. They got someone over at Puddletown they sell them to.

Frank says the gentry only got themselves to blame. They won't never miss the odd bird or two, he says. I tell him to be careful the gamekeepers don't catch them. Father would die of shame if that happened. But Frank don't listen to me now like he used to.

If you was still with us, Alice, I'm sure he wouldn't never be so bad . . .

3rd October 1925

. . . At the Harvest Supper this evening I sang one of the hymns:

Bright robes of gold the fields adorn,
The hills with joy are ringing,
The valleys stand so thick with corn
That even they are singing.

In the middle of it, I caught sight of Father's dahlias helping decorate the hall. Red and orange and yellow, beautiful bright colours. I felt so fond of Father just at that minute I couldn't hardly sing.

Sir Wilfred sat at the top of the table with Lady

Emily. He made a speech and everybody clapped. But then Lady Emily got up and made a speech too . . .

Lady Emily is tall and very thin. She wears a long grey skirt and jacket and a mauve hat.

She stands and looks down the long table at the two lines of upturned faces; at the sheaves of wheat and the piles of tomatoes and marrows; at the burning colours of the dahlias.

She starts to speak of the fields and gardens of Lansbury Abbas being full of golden harvest, to tell the villagers that they must be thankful to God for His treasures. But then somehow she is talking of the war, and of all the young men cut down, as a cornfield is cut down. Millions and millions of young men.

'Cut down,' she repeats, 'cut down,' and her hands twist round and round each other . . .

None of us didn't know what to do. Sir Wilfred pulled at her skirt and at last Lady Emily sat down and people began talking again.

But I saw Lady Emily's hands and they was shaking . . .

'Goodness, darling,' exclaimed Hilary, standing in the open doorway with her muddy shoes in her hand. 'Aren't you cold out here? What've you been doing?'

'Reading.' Joanna put the notebook in her pocket.

'Must have been something interesting. Look what I've got.' She dug in her jacket pockets and brought out two little bottles of cider and two bags of crisps.

'Hey, Mum, I thought you'd been on a great country walk.'

'I have. That's the sort of walk you have in the country. Up to the end of the lane, dodging the puddles, along the main road to the village, dodging the cars, and into the nearest pub.'

'Dodging the guys who try and pick you up.'

'What an old-fashioned girl you are, Jo. The Partridge Inn is the centre of life in Lansbury Abbas. Most respectable. I've learned all about the Youth Club, and the Women's Institute . . .'

She shepherded Joanna inside and shut the door.

'The Youth Club was closed down recently, I'm afraid. They couldn't find anyone willing to be the leader. But the W.I. is flourishing. I've said I'll probably join it next month.'

Humming, she went into the kitchen to put on the kettle. Joanna stared after her.

She hadn't thought before that Hilary might be finding it lonely in Dorset. She'd been too busy herself coping with leaving London for a new home and school really to have noticed Hilary at all.

But, thinking back to how Mum used to be in London, she remembered how she was always rushing round, helping organise a school bazaar or a sponsored swim, going out for the evening with Dad or with her physiotherapist friends, playing badminton. Violet Bottom, alone with Joanna day after day, might have seemed incredibly dull after that.

'Know what I saw up in the village, Jo?' Hilary called from the kitchen. 'A real Thomas Hardy scene. This crowd of youngsters sitting on the War Memorial steps with a radio blaring, cigarettes in their mouths, bottles in their hands and half a dozen motor bikes racing round and round. And who do you think was in the middle of it? Your friend Vivien Dennis.'

'Not my friend, Mum.'

'Oh. Well, I must say I saw her a bit differently tonight. No wonder the Youth Club closed down. Would that be why you gave up the school bus?'

'Partly.'

'Still,' said Hilary. 'We've got to keep battling on, haven't we, Jo? Making the best of it here?' There was an almost pleading note to her voice.

'Oh, sure, yes.'

Nobody made me come, Joanna thought. I said I'd move to Dorset with Mum and start a new life and I'm doing it. It was no use staying with Dad; he's completely hopeless. And I'm going to make it work.

I've made a start. Cycling to school instead of going by bus is a start. Not letting people like Vivien push me around is a start. Being in charge of my own life.

That's the secret. Knowing what you want in life and going for it, whatever it takes.

Like Jessie Bone . . .

. . . Sometimes I almost frighten myself when I'm singing. I feel so much joy. I'm lifted up, not quite in myself no more.

I can't explain, Alice, even to you. It's the music. When I get it just right . . . It fills me with power . . .

Chapter Fourteen

The weather changed once more. The rain clouds moved away; the skies cleared. There were long days of hot sun. Joanna, cycling to school in the mornings, felt it beat down on her back. By her journey home again in the afternoons it was almost unbearable. The soil dried out and, surprisingly quickly, the fresh green of the grass verges began to turn brown.

At school, a lethargy had settled on everyone. Those unlucky enough to have exams went through them grimly, but for the rest the pace slowed. Lessons were given in classrooms cooled into shady caverns by drawn blinds. In lunch hours, even the youngest pupils sat quietly outside instead of rushing round playing games, and the PE staff allowed their students to take things a little more easily.

Except Mr Sharman.

Joanna had known from that basketball session with him on her first day at the school that Mr Sharman was not the sort of man to let his energies slacken simply because of the heat. If anything, he seemed to expect them to work harder.

'Next . . . next . . . next . . .' Joanna at the head of the line felt his hand between her shoulder-blades push her forward and she began to run, stumbling a little on the dry hard ground.

'Next . . .' Becky followed, then Leela. 'Next . . . next . . . next . . .' Mr Sharman was the only PE teacher to insist in this hot weather that everyone run right round the field before starting any other sort of outdoor activity.

'Slavedriver,' panted Becky. Joanna slowed to allow her to catch up. Becky's face was shiny with heat. 'That man's nothing but a sadist. He enjoys seeing us sweat.'

'Keep going, you two.' Mr Sharman cupped his hands round his mouth to shout across the field. 'You're not gossiping in the hairdresser's. Get on with it, Becky love. And you, Jo-Jo.'

Jo-Jo. Joanna stood still. Leela, coming from behind, nearly cannoned into her.

'What's the matter?'

Perhaps it was the heat. Perhaps it was remembering Jessie, who'd always been treated with respect.

'You heard what he called me. He's picked that up from Vivien or somebody. And calling everyone "love" like that. I'm going to tell him.' Joanna started to walk back again. 'It's patronising.'

'Lots of people call you "love". They don't mean any harm.'

'Sharman does,' Joanna said. 'He's using it to put us down. It's time somebody told him.'

'Hey.' Mr Sharman ran up, flapping his arms at them. 'Did I say you could stop? You keep running. You might lose some of that weight, Becky love.'

'Mr Sharman,' Joanna said.

Mr Sharman glanced at her. 'What now?'

Joanna swallowed. A knot of curious people had started to gather round. 'Mr Sharman, my name's Joanna. Not Jo-Jo.'

She saw Vivien and Paul exchange grins. With an effort, she managed to keep looking the teacher in the eyes.

'We don't like the way you speak to us sometimes.' Joanna could hear her own voice, sounding pompous and absurd. 'Using nicknames and things.'

He stared at her in silence. His dark eyes were without expression.

'Well, tough,' he said at last. His glance flicked round the rest of the group. 'Where's your sense of humour?'

'It's not funny.'

Joanna jerked her head round. It was Richard

Horsefield who'd spoken.

'Not always.' He was very red in the face.

'I think you ought to –' Leela began.

Mr Sharman's jaw tightened. 'I'm not having advice from you. Now, get back running. All of you.'

For a moment, nobody moved. Then two or three people turned and jogged away round the field and the group broke up. Mr Sharman strode off.

'Sorry, Jo,' Becky said. 'I wasn't much help.'

'That's OK.' Joanna smiled a bit shakily. 'It was my thing, not yours. And I don't suppose it's done any good.'

'You wait and see,' Richard said. 'Sharman's not used to people telling him where he gets off. At least you've given him something to think about.'

Chapter Fifteen

Cycling home from school that afternoon past Ennington Country Park, and seeing the gates standing open, Joanna suddenly decided to go in. Her mother worked longer in the afternoons now, so as long as she was home by six it would be all right.

She cycled past the nine-hole golf course and the start of the little narrow-gauge scenic railway that took visitors round the park, and just glimpsed the lake away over on her left before a bend in the drive brought her the first view of Ennington Hall.

So this was the Big House that the villagers of the nineteen-twenties had known. It stood grey and foursquare in a hollow of the parkland. It had three floors of large regularly placed sash windows and, above that, a row of smaller attic windows jutted from the grey slate roof. Minna Kellaway and the other servants had once slept up there.

A white stone balustrade ran right round the edge of the roof, and above the chimneys a red and white flag of St George flapped lazily in the heat.

Joanna squinted into the sun, trying to imagine Jessie's father working up there, often in the freezing cold, sawing blocks of stone to repair the balustrade, or checking that the chimneys were still sound after a gale had swept through the Park.

But whatever his usual tasks had been, something new and unexpected had been given to him soon after that Harvest Supper in 1925. Joanna had read about it in the green notebook:

> . . . Sir Wilfred's idea, something to help Lady Emily

feel better about Mr Raymond dying in the Great War.

They're going to build a memorial to him, down by the lake.

There'll be paths and grottoes and fountains, and a flight of steps leading up through the trees to a big stone cross at the top with Mr Raymond's name on it.

A famous architect from London is designing it all and they're bringing in lots of workmen. And – guess what, Alice? Sir Wilfred and Lady Emily have insisted that Father should be the foreman in charge.

I wish you could have seen him last night. He was so happy, happier than I've ever seen him. I cleared away the supper things and he sketched everything out for us. He couldn't talk about nothing else all evening.

It'll be hard work, because it has to be finished by 1st July next year. That'll be the tenth anniversary of the day Mr Raymond was killed at the Battle of the Somme. There'll be a big ceremony, with lots of guests and a bishop to dedicate it and Father in the front row, I should think . . .

Joanna fastened her bicycle securely to some railings and turned towards the house. The front doors stood wide open and she went inside, grateful for the sudden coolness of the marble entrance hall.

Lady Emily and Sir Wilfred and their servants must have gone backwards and forwards all day across this hall, in and out of the rooms that led off it. Miss Pamela and her friends would have run up and down that graceful staircase soaring out of sight to the floors above, and their voices would have filled the whole house with life.

Now the hall and the adjoining rooms just housed a wildlife exhibition, and a rope had been stretched across the bottom of the stairs to stop visitors going up there.

Back in the blazing sunshine Joanna set out down one of the paths. It wasn't the house she'd come to see.

3rd December 1925
. . . Even in these winter days, Father's working hard on the Memorial Walk, as it's to be called.

He says that Lady Emily visits the site every single day, whatever the weather. She sits there for hours, watching them work and gazing across the lake . . .

Memorial Walk. The name was carved on one of the little wooden signposts, together with Adventure Playground, Nature Trail and The Lake. Joanna could see the lake more clearly now, a smooth silver-grey sheet of water half hidden by the trees. She crossed a cattle grid, followed a narrow path across a field and came to a little swing gate that led through to the lakeside.

It was here that George Bone and his workmen had set out to construct the Memorial Walk for Sir Wilfred and Lady Emily, in memory of their only son. It began at the point where Joanna now stood, with a hump-backed bridge crossing the stream that fed into the lake from the water meadows beyond. Carved on the parapet of the bridge was an oak leaf and acorn, and the initials R.V.M., and this emblem was repeated at intervals along the stone wall that followed the lake edge towards the grottoes:

. . . Lady Emily wants Father to carve Mr Raymond's initials on everything he builds in the Memorial Walk, and he's got to put acorns too. She says that acorns fall into the ground, but they aren't really lost. Sometimes they grow up again into great oak trees. That's how she thinks of Mr Raymond, she told Father. Not lost, but still growing somewhere. It's a nice idea. I like to think about it too, Alice, for you . . .

* * *

Joanna walked quietly along the Memorial Walk. On her left the sun was shimmering on the lake, but the trees growing on her right threw stripes of shade across the paved path and the seats where people rested from the heat. Golden roses and white ones, planted here long ago, clung to George Bone's stone walls and today the air was heavy with their scent.

Then the path entered the first grotto. There were three of them, small artificial caves linked by the path, hollowed out of the hillside and furnished with stone seats. Again, the acorn emblem and initials were carved on the walls.

Emerging from the last grotto, Joanna came to the centrepiece of the memorial, a circular paved area with fountains and flowerbeds and, rising from it, a flight of steps leading up through the trees.

Joanna hesitated. It was very hot. But somehow she felt she owed it to Jessie to make the effort and perhaps, obscurely, to Lady Emily as well. She began to climb.

Sixty-five, sixty-six, sixty-seven . . . Breathless, she came to the top. And there was the cross that Jessie had mentioned, rising tall and slender against the blue sky, with a wreath of acorns and oak leaves carved around the brief inscription:

R.V.M.
1897 – 1916
There everlasting spring abides

Joanna went down again to sit in the coolness of the grottoes. She remembered those last few words; they came from 'There Is a Land of Pure Delight' which Jessie had sung on the day she left school in 1924. And Lady Emily had cried.

She took out the green notebook from her bag. It would be rather good to read about the Memorial Walk being finished and about the dedication ceremony while she was actually on the spot. She began to flip through the pages. Jessie seemed to be working harder than ever as 1925 drew to a close:

> 11th December 1925
> ...We've been doing three more dance dresses for Dr Tripp's daughters. I went with Miss Mountain yesterday to a fitting in a house near Bere Regis. She wouldn't let me do much, just pass her the pins and write down the measurements, but the house was lovely. A parlourmaid let us in and they had really thick carpets and big warm fires everywhere ...

> 26th February 1926
> ...Yesterday Mrs Kellaway went out for an hour up to the village. As soon as she'd gone, I dropped my sewing and made for the piano. Mr Cadwallader's given me a very difficult song to learn, and I need – oh, Alice – I need more time. Will I ever be able just to work and work on my singing? No more meals to cook, or washing to do, or any more dresses to make, just singing ...

Always singing. It was as if Jessie was beginning to get tunnel vision, as if nothing else mattered to her except her ambition to become a famous singer. Only rarely did the outside world touch her:

> 10th May 1926
> ...The General Strike's been on a week now. Minna says Miss Pamela's friends in London are working on the trams, and they think it's an absolute scream. But I met Mr Mahler today and he says the workers must stay out, their conditions are dreadful ...

There must be something about the Memorial Walk. Oh, yes, here it was:

20th May 1926

... I was out in the garden when Father came home, very late and tired. At last he admitted he was worried about the Memorial Walk. The architect had been down to see it and there was a big meeting. The weather has held everything up, and there's less than eight weeks to go now. Father says there's still so much to do ...

25th May 1926

... They're working later and later into the evenings. The steps are still half to do, and a lot of the carving. I asked Father if anybody else could help with the carving, but he said of course not. You know what Father's like, Alice. He's got to get it perfect. If only the rain would stop ...

30th May 1926

... Sunday morning. Father's one day of rest. I wanted him to stay home from church, but he just went on polishing his boots and didn't answer. I don't think he's ever missed church in his whole life.

In the service, he nodded off several times and I had to wake him. Then, coming out at the end, Sir Wilfred stopped us. He sent Lady Emily to wait in the car, and he stood talking to Father in the church porch. I don't know what they said; Father wouldn't tell me, but they talked for a long time.

All afternoon Father sat at home reading his Bible. He wouldn't rest. As usual on Sunday nights, he asked me to play some hymns and to sing. But even after we'd gone to bed, I could hear him pacing about. I'm starting to get frightened, Alice ...

Joanna glanced at her watch. She really ought to go home. She turned the page:

I hate him . . . I hate him . . . How can Father do this to me? Alice, I can't bear it, I can't . . .

Joanna stared, wide-eyed. The words were scrawled in a thick black pencil, quite unlike Jessie's usual careful ink script. But it was her writing all right:

Father has ruined my life. I'll never be a great singer now. Alice, help me, tell me what to do, Alice.

He's stopped my singing lessons. He sat down at the table this evening and wrote a letter to Mr Cadwallader, saying the lessons must end at once. Then he went straight out of the house with the letter to walk to Lansbury Abbas and post it.

Why? Why, Alice?

Because he won't work on a Sunday.

Sir Wilfred decided they must all work the next four Sundays, to get the Memorial Walk finished by 1st July. He offered them extra money. Everybody else agreed.

Father was the only one to refuse.

He told us this evening. That's what Sir Wilfred was talking to him about yesterday in the church porch, saying it was only for four weeks, saying it was for Lady Emily's sake, so the dedication ceremony wouldn't be spoilt.

Father asked for time to think it over.

And today he told Sir Wilfred he couldn't do it. Better to have the work unfinished than to spoil it in God's eyes, he said. He told him the Bible said: *Remember the Sabbath day to keep it holy.* He said sorry if Lady Emily were disappointed, but he couldn't do it. His conscience wouldn't let him.

So Sir Wilfred dismissed him.

Father come home at four o'clock, carrying all his tools. He's hung them up in the wash house. The London architect will bring in another foreman at once, and they'll work every day of the week now and make sure it's ready on 1st July for the ceremony.

Father's got to start looking for work. Sir Wilfred will let him buy the lease of the cottage, so we can still live here. But it will cost £130 and he wants the money quickly.

Father says we must all make sacrifices. He may never get another job at his age, and he's relying on us.

So Harold give him the money he was saving to get married next year. Then Frank offered to do without the motor bike he wanted. And Leonard said he'd take a market stall every Saturday so he could sell vegetables and eggs.

Then they all looked at me . . .

Alice, I couldn't. In the end, Father came out with it, asking me to give up my lessons, saying my singing weren't so important as keeping a roof over our heads, saying he must have more of my earnings than I'd been giving

And I said no, that I'd give anything else but that. I told him my lessons are my whole life, my whole future.

He just looked at me. Then he sat down and wrote that letter to Mr Cadwallader and went out to post it . .

The door closes on George Bone. His four children go on sitting round the kitchen table. Nobody speaks.

Then Harold laces his long fingers and looks at Jessie.

'It's my money,' she says. 'My money. I earn it sewing, week after week —'

'We all earn money.' His voice is cold. 'And we got a duty to Father.'

'I *need* it.' Her hair falls across her face. 'To be a singer.'

Frank leans forward. 'Jess, you can be a singer if you

wants to. You got a lovely voice. You don't need no fancy lessons –'

'Stupid!' She bangs the table. 'I'll need lessons for years. Years and years of work. Why don't nobody understand – ?'

'Stupid, is it?'

It's Leonard. Silent, self-sufficient young Leonard. His face is flushed as he looks at his sister.

'You're the one what's stupid. You think Father didn't feel bad saying that to you? Why d'you think he went straight out to post that letter? Because he's afraid he might not post it at all if he don't, that's why. And you th-th –'

He stutters on the words. 'You think Father don't understand what work is? When he comes home with his hands all torn and bleeding, and he's too tired to stand up sometimes, and still he comes out and helps me in the garden? You –' His voice, full of scorn, cracks slightly.

'You don't know what work is, sitting there with a bit of sewing, singing songs at the piano –'

Jessie pushes back her chair with a crash, and runs upstairs to her father's room. The door slams.

In the kitchen there's silence.

. . . It's nearly midnight. The boys have gone to bed and Father'll be back from the village very soon. He'll creep in and not notice I've gone.

Because I'm not staying in this house another minute.

All I ever wanted was to be a singer so you'd be proud of me, Alice. I don't care about nothing now. Nothing.

I can't write no more, Alice. I'm going out.

Your loving, heartbroken sister
Jessie.

Chapter Sixteen

Decaffeinated coffee . . .

Joanna looked at her mother's shopping list helplessly. Nothing on it quite fitted with the things on the shelves in front of her.

Oh, well, she thought. It's only the village shop. We'll have to go to a supermarket in Blandford or Dorchester to get half these things, though I bet we'll spend twice as much if we do.

She dropped a jar of ordinary coffee in her wire basket and moved towards the checkout.

'Oh, hello, Miss Kellaway.'

The old lady turned round and smiled.

'How's things down at Violet Bottom?' she asked. 'Any news of Leonard?'

'No,' said Joanna. 'But I'm looking after his budgie.'

Miss Kellaway fumbled in her purse. 'There we are, Jim.'

'Ta, my love.'

It was odd, Joanna thought, that this time 'love' didn't sound patronising, as it always did when Mr Sharman said it to the girls in his classes.

'Mind how you go now.'

'I will.'

She moved painfully slowly, edging her walking frame forward little by little, her shopping bag dangling from one handle. When Joanna came out into the sunny street, she'd only gone a few metres.

'Miss Kellaway.'

'Just a moment, dear.' She lowered herself on to a bench opposite the War Memorial.

'That's better. I'll be all right now till the bus comes. I

like to pop out when I can to get my bits and pieces.'

'About Jessie Bone . . .'

The faded blue eyes became guarded. 'What about her?'

'Well – ' Joanna perched on the end of the seat. 'Do you remember a time she was angry with her father? When he lost his job at the Big House and he stopped her singing lessons?'

She waited. The village was busy this Saturday morning, people squeezing their cars in any available spaces against the cottages that lined the street. A poster on the churchyard wall said: COFFEE MORNING IN THE RECTORY TODAY. She wondered if Vivien would be there in her little-pink-frock-Rector's-daughter mood, or if she'd escaped from the whole thing with her motor-bike friends.

'Miss Kellaway?'

The old lady said, 'Jess had a bad time then. Those singing lessons meant everything to her, and her dad just cut them off without no warning. But he had to do it. He thought he might never get another job. The unemployment was dreadful then.'

'I know. Like it is today.'

She shook her head fiercely. 'There weren't all the Social Security you get now. And Jessie's dad stood to lose the cottage if he didn't buy it quick. They'd have had no roof over their heads. They could've ended up in the workhouse.'

'Oh, I see.'

Everyone had been asked to make sacrifices. But Jessie wouldn't.

'Miss Kellaway, what happened that night when he stopped the lessons? Didn't Jessie go running out of the house?'

Her head snapped round. 'Who told you that?'

Joanna nearly said, 'Jessie did. Or rather, she told Alice.

104

But she never told her what happened after she ran out. She didn't write to Alice again for weeks.'

Impossible to say that to Minna Kellaway, so she said instead, 'Oh, I heard something about it, you know how it is.'

Surprisingly, that worked. Miss Kellaway began to talk.

It had been the first of June, 1926, very early in the morning. Minna had got up as usual at the Big House and started her daily routine of cleaning out fireplaces. At about half-past six she'd gone across the back courtyard to empty the ashcan and Jessie had been there, standing in the shadows of one of the outbuildings.

'Oh, she did give me a turn. I couldn't think why she were there. She said she'd been out all night, just wandering round the Park, round and round all night, looking at things.'

Looking at her father's work on the Memorial Walk. Asking herself which was more important: George Bone's principles about not working on Sundays, or her own career as a singer . . .

The moon edges out for a moment from behind a cloud and the house in the hollow of the Park is thrown into pale relief. Its chimneys and low stone balustrade running round the top of the roof are silhouetted against the pool of sudden cool light in the sky. Then the clouds close in once more and darkness pours back like the sea.

Horses stamp in the stable; in the kennels, the hunting dogs dream. Animals and birds crouch in the undergrowth, bright-eyed, scanning the darkness for enemies.

Some young poachers lie flat on their stomachs, waiting. A gamekeeper has just passed by on his rounds, unaware that they are there only metres from the path.

The young men, in their turn, do not know that another

person is moving round the grounds of Ennington Hall this summer night. Jessie Bone is crossing a field, her feet silent on the grass.

She passes through the little swing gate that leads to the lakeside, over the hump-backed bridge and on along the path where a newly built wall borders the water. She hesitates before moving through the three small grottoes and emerging on the far side. But here her way is blocked. The path ends abruptly in a rough hole and a heap of stones. Ahead of her, a half-completed flight of steps vanishes upwards through a slash in the trees.

She puts out a hand to the wall and fingers the carved acorns and initials R.V.M.

'Father,' she whispers. 'Father.'

Somewhere in the woods, an owl glides low and a rabbit screams . . .

'She were shivering,' said Miss Kellaway, 'and so pale. Oh, she did take things hard, poor Jess. I knew she'd come to find me because she were afraid to go home by then. I mean, only sixteen and stopping out all night. Maybe you think that's nothing today, but then – '

She shook her head. 'We couldn't neither of us think what her dad would do if he found out.'

'And did he?'

'Jess were so unlucky,' said Miss Kellaway. 'I thought if she hurried home she might creep in before her dad got up. After all, he wouldn't be going to work. If it hadn't been for Frank . . .'

'Frank?'

The old lady looked along the road to see if the bus was coming.

'Jessie's brother Frank,' she said. 'He were out that night too.'

'Oh,' said Joanna. 'Oh, I see.'

Frank had gone out poaching at Ennington Hall, as he

often did. But this time when he came back, Jessie wasn't there to let him in. Joanna pictured him knocking at the window and calling, trying to be quiet but growing more and more alarmed.

'His father heard him in the end and came down. And then – oh, my word, what an upset – they realised Jess weren't there.'

'They must have been worried.'

'Worried out of their minds,' said Miss Kellaway. 'And not only that. Her dad were angry. First he loses his job. Then his daughter's gone out at night. To top it all, he catches his son poaching, from the Big House of all places. Because of course he got the whole story out of Frank in five minutes. Frank weren't one to tell lies.' Her face softened a little. 'You could never say that of Frank.'

'I'm surprised he went poaching that night,' Joanna said, 'when he knew his father had just lost his job.'

'Ah, but he were trying to help, see. That's what he told me afterwards. The arrangements was already made, and Frank thought he'd make some money and give it all to his dad. Give you anything, Frank would. And he wanted to get back at Sir Wilfred for the way he'd treated his dad.' She sounded shocked.

'And Jessie?'

'Oh, such a hue and cry. They woke my mother first, in case Jess'd gone next door to her. But she'd never have done that. She didn't go to other people with her troubles.'

'She went to you,' Joanna pointed out.

Miss Kellaway smiled sadly. 'Yes, but what could I do? I got her some milk from the kitchen when nobody weren't looking, and I tried to talk to her, but I could see she weren't listening. Then I had to go back to work or I'd have been in trouble. So Jess said she'd go home.'

'And did she?'

Where else could she have gone? Minna's mother had seen her coming along the lane, dragging her feet, her head down. George Bone and Jessie's three brothers had been searching the fields round Violet Bottom for hours. Harold was about to cycle up to the village to get the policeman. Then she came back.

'And then?'

Minna Kellaway turned and gazed at Joanna, blinking a little.

'No more. Mother told me later that Harold said in his sharpest sort of voice, *Jessie, how could you?* But Leonard – and he were a big boy of thirteen or so by this time – he done something Mother'd never seen him do since he were a little tiddler. He went over to Jess and put his arms right round her.'

'What about her father?'

She sighed. 'He never said a word. He just turned round and went into the house. And they all followed him in and shut the door. And that's all I can tell you, my dear.'

Chapter Seventeen

Who could say what had gone on behind the closed door of Number One, Violet Bottom? Even with Jessie's letters to Alice in front of her, Joanna found it hard to piece the whole story together. The Bone family seemed simply to have closed in on itself, as it had when Alice had died, undisturbed by any outsider.

Except by Mr Tom Mahler.

30th June 1926

Dearest Alice,

More than four weeks since I've written. I just wanted to tell you. Mr Mahler come round last night.

I seen him striding down the lane with his black beard bristling, and I knew he'd heard about the lessons.

He talked to Father in the parlour. I was in the kitchen doing some washing.

'Good God, man,' I heard, 'I'll give you the money myself.' Then I knew it were hopeless.

'I'll ask you not to use the name of the Lord in that way, sir,' Father said. 'Now, if that's all you got to say . . .'

Mr Mahler come out, red in the face, ramming his hat back on his head, muttering about a wicked waste of talent.

I ran out before Father shut the door and caught him up. He stood still in the lane waiting for me.

'Jessie,' he says. 'I tried.'

I said I knew that and I thanked him.

'Such stubborn pride.' I could see he were really angry. 'When the money's being offered to him . . .'

I told him Father don't change his mind once it's made up. Never. Not when he thinks what he's doing is right.

'Then you must be just as strong,' says Mr Mahler, his eyes looking right into mine. 'Don't give up, Jessie, whatever happens. Don't you never give up.'

Harold was coming along the lane. He passed us by with scarcely a nod to Mr Mahler and went in the house. Mr Mahler walked off up the lane. And I were left stood there by myself.

Today I had a nice note from Mr Cadwallader, saying he were sorry I wouldn't be coming for lessons no more . . .

2nd July 1926

. . . Frank brought the newspaper home with him tonight, full of pictures of the Memorial Walk. It said:

'Thanks to the devoted work of all who laboured for long hours on this magnificent tribute to a fallen son, who perished with 19,000 of his comrades in the mud and agony of the Somme on a single morning ten years ago, a family and a village has been able to mourn their loss with dignity and pride.'

There was a photo of the fountains playing and of Lady Emily, Sir Wilfred and Miss Pamela at the top of the steps, staring at the cross with Mr Raymond's name on. Down below, almost everybody in the village stood and watched and, the paper said, 'drank in the beauty of the whole wonderful completed concept'.

We hid the paper under my workbasket when we heard Father come home. He'd been out looking for work all day . . .

21st September 1926

. . . Father heard of a building job over near Wimborne yesterday, miles away. He cycled off at

110

once but of course it'd gone when he got there. Over a hundred people were asking about it, they said.

Leonard's boots need mending. Frank says he'll do them. Father helps Leonard now with the market stall . . .

3rd October 1926

. . .The piano tuner called today. I let him in and he sat down at the piano to begin, but Father come in then and sent him away, saying he was afraid we wouldn't be needing him no more. He looked very sorry when he left. He's been coming to us ever since Mother were alive and used to play the piano . . .

24th October 1926

. . . I'm in trouble again with Father. I can't do nothing right lately. He were digging in the garden and he heard me playing the piano when I should've been next door sewing.

He said if I've got time to play the piano I can ask Miss Mountain for more work, and I ought to be thinking about starting training in dressmaking. He said music's a nice little hobby, but learning a trade's the most important thing in life.

I tried to tell him it weren't, not in my life, but he walked off and wouldn't answer . . .

7th November 1926

. . . Father's been working on a farm, cleaning out ditches. He gets paid twelve and six a week. It's only for two weeks.

The farmer's taken Frank on too. He said he might keep him for good if he works hard and don't expect to be paid much, but not Father, not at his age.

Frank told me he's really going to settle down. No more visits to the Big House at nights . . .

111

4th December 1926

... Father has a bad chest so I went to the market with Leonard this morning. We sold most of the Brussels sprouts and swedes but too many other stalls had carrots and potatoes. We got very cold.

Leonard bought us a mug of tea and that kept us going till the afternoon ...

Joanna sighed, and closed the notebook. She needed some fresh air. She'd go and help Mum in the garden for an hour or two before the weekend was over, or the weeds would take control completely.

'Hey, Jo, one of these? Hang on, I'll get it for you.'

The ninth year were running a tuck shop on Monday morning, raising money for Cancer Research. People jostled round the tables in Break, holding out their money.

'OK?' Breathless, Becky backed out of the crowd, her arms laden with snacks and cans of drink.

'Leela . . . Jo . . . that's 85p you owe me. Thanks.'

The three girls retreated to a corner.

'What are you doing at the weekend, Jo? Anything nice?'

'Nothing special.'

Joanna couldn't think of a way of telling them it was her birthday on Saturday. It might sound as if she was asking for cards or presents. Anyway, she wasn't doing anything special on Saturday.

She could have been, of course. She could have been in London for the weekend.

Suddenly a longing for London swept through her, for the taxis and red buses and the underground trains, for the feeling that you'd never, never see everything there was to see because there was so much to choose from. She and her friend Paula Rossi used to dash about by underground all over the city, up at one station and down again at another, talking, laughing, looking at things.

But she didn't want to be in London with her father. There'd been a time when he'd been good fun. But not now.

'Morning, girls. Not eating again, Becky love?'

Becky froze, a Mars Bar halfway to her mouth.

'She'll do great things for her figure, won't she, lads?' Mr Sharman appealed to the bystanders. 'Getting big and busty, eh, Richard, Paul? Very tasty, our Becky's going to be if she goes on like –'

'Mr *Sharman* . . .'

It wasn't just Joanna this time. It was Leela and Becky herself too. They all three turned and glared at him.

'Oh,' Mr Sharman mimed terror, 'what have I done?'

'Joanna told you before,' Becky said. 'We don't like the way you talk sometimes.'

His face darkened, became sulky.

'I'm a PE teacher. Right? My job is to advise you on diet and fitness. Are you telling me I don't know my job?'

'No,' said Leela. 'We're asking you to speak to us with . . . with . . .'

'Respect,' said Joanna. The last time she'd stood up to Mr Sharman it had made her feel shaky inside, but not this time. Now she felt calm and sure.

'Respect us, Mr Sharman, and we'll respect you.'

18th December 1926

Father met a builder in Dorchester yesterday he used to know. He told Father to come and see him after Christmas.

Does it mean a proper job at last? Father says that God will guide him into the right path in His own good time . . .

22nd December 1926

Mr Mahler wanted to get up a group to go carol singing round the village last night. I didn't want to go but in the end I did.

Frank said we ought to go up the Big House, that they'd give us plenty of money. Mr Mahler wouldn't go. Everyone knows he don't approve of the gentry. Father says Mr Mahler's a socialist and he'd get rid of the gentry if he could.

Instead, we sang outside Bert Tapper's cottage because he's been ill. We didn't know Lady Emily were inside visiting him till she come out and listened. And she give Mr Mahler a *pound* for his collection. He were so cross. But he had to take it . . .

30th December 1926

Father went to see the builder, and he's come back with a job!

But, Alice, it's only builder's labourer. He won't need his tools, he'll be pushing barrows and mixing mortar. And the wages aren't half as good as he got at the Big House, only eleven pence an hour, maybe going up to a shilling an hour in a year. But it's better than nothing. And now perhaps I won't have to do that extra sewing.

I'm glad to see the end of 1926, everything's so different from this time last year . . .

3rd January 1927

. . . Oh, Alice, do you think 1927 could be a new start?

I were in the village. A motor stopped and Lady Emily leaned out. She asked me about my singing, saying she noticed me the other night with the carol singers. So I had to tell her Father had stopped my lessons, months ago, when he lost his job. And now our piano is badly out of tune.

She didn't say nothing for a long time. Sir Wilfred just sat there, staring in front of him.

Then she said, 'We must respect one another.

Without respect we are nothing.'
I said, 'Beg pardon, my lady?'
But she didn't answer. Instead she said, 'I believe
you do sewing for Miss Mountain. I'll be asking her
to make me one or two coats and skirts shortly, and I
would like you to accompany her for the fittings at
the Hall. I have something I wish to say to you, Jessie.'
Before I could answer, Sir Wilfred had tapped the
chauffeur on the shoulder and they'd gone. Oh, Alice,
what can it be she wants to tell me . . .?

For the rest of the day after the tuck shop incident with Mr
Sharman, Joanna sat through lessons and thought about
Jessie Bone.

If people were going to respect you, to let you be
yourself, you had to be strong. Even when Jessie's life had
seemed to be collapsing around her, she'd still held on to
what she wanted. She wouldn't give up.

So, if Joanna wanted friends, she was going to have to
do something about it, not just sit about hoping to be
noticed.

She waited until they were in the locker room packing
up to go home. Then she went over to Becky and Leela and
invited them to Violet Bottom for the day on Saturday to
help her celebrate her birthday.

'Yes, great. Love to.'

'It'll only be Mum and me,' Joanna warned, 'and it's
right out in the country. But if you haven't got anything
better to do . . .'

'My mum'll be delighted,' Becky said. 'She's always
saying I hang around at weekends doing nothing, eating
too much.'

'Building up that tasty figure,' said Joanna. ''Bye.'

On her way to the bike sheds she passed Vivien Dennis,
on her own for once. Joanna was feeling so good that, just
for a second, she nearly invited Vivien for her birthday as

well. Then she squashed the idea firmly.

It's possible to go right over the top. It's only in books you can go and be nice to the worst person you know and they're suddenly transformed into your best friend.

In real life, there are people you'll never be friends with, and you might as well accept it.

Chapter Eighteen

7th February 1927

Dearest Alice,

Something so wonderful . . . You could never guess. Ever since Father stopped my lessons, I've been praying for . . . something, I didn't know what. Just some way I could go on with my music, and not forget everything that Mr Cadwallader taught me.

And now it's happened, it's like a miracle. The strangest thing is, Alice, it were the sewing led to it. Who'd ever believe that sewing could lead to anything so wonderful . . .?

Lady Emily turns slowly in front of the looking glass. 'I think, Miss Mountain,' she says, 'that will do quite well. What is your opinion, Robbins?'

Her maid inclines her head. 'Most elegant, my lady.'

Jessie Bone, crouching at Lady Emily's feet with a mouthful of pins, glances up at Miss Mountain.

'Yes, you may complete the hem, Jessie.' Miss Mountain, a tiny woman in spite of her name, hovers behind Lady Emily. 'Take care, now.'

'Yes, Miss Mountain.' Jessie edges forward on her knees, measuring and putting in a line of pins.

'Now, Miss Mountain, a cup of tea . . .'

Miss Mountain flutters her pleasure. 'Thank you, my lady.'

'Robbins will show you. Thank you, Robbins.'

'My lady.'

As they go out, the two women glance back at Jessie, still busy on the floor. Quietly she continues fastening the hem.

'Jessie. Have you finished?'

'Yes, my lady.' She replaces the unused pins in her pincushion. 'That were the last one.'

'Was,' says Lady Emily. 'That was the last one. Now come with me.'

She goes out into the long corridor and Jessie follows. At the far end is a staircase and, at the top, another corridor. Jessie's right shoe creaks a little as she walks, and she turns her foot slightly to try to stop it.

Lady Emily comes to a door and pauses, looking Jessie up and down. Then she nods to herself and turns the handle. The room is full of light, the February sun streaming in at the large windows overlooking the Park.

'The piano.' Lady Emily puts out a hand to the gleaming wood. '*His* piano.'

There are music stands and metronomes. Thick rugs glow on the polished floor. Shelves hold piles of carefully arranged sheet music.

Jessie stares. She doesn't speak.

'Well, Jessie?' There is a trace of impatience now in Lady Emily's voice. 'Don't you understand?'

Her eyes go to a portrait on the wall. 'This room belonged to my son, Mr Raymond. He worked on his music here for many, many hours until he – went away. Since then, it has not been used. But now, Jessie –'

She crosses to the piano and raises the lid carefully.

'I want you to come here whenever you wish. It is time there was music in this room again . . .'

. . . I don't think, Alice, I said thank you at all. I just stood there, and looked. And all I could say was, 'Oh, my lady . . .'

Not a *party*, Joanna thought, sitting on the front doorstep, rubbing her hair with a towel. I only asked them to come here for the day. A day sounded an awful long time to spend with Becky and Leela. She hardly knew them really. She put down the towel and began combing out her hair, lifting her face to the sun. On this hot windless morning the whole view shimmered with a bluish haze.

It didn't feel much like her birthday, although Mum had tried hard at breakfast, and cards and presents had arrived by post. She'd stayed awake last night reading some more of Jessie's letters, and today she felt a bit headachy and tired, Jessie's thoughts weaving in and out with her own.

'Coffee, Jo?' Hilary called from the kitchen. 'Or a cold drink?'

'Not till they come. It'll be something to do then.'

Probably they'd phone in a minute to say they weren't coming, that Leela's mother hadn't been able to find the place and they were giving up and going home.

Joanna found herself quite cheered up by this idea. She and Mum could lie around in the shade reading, eating all the lunch. Then they could go into Dorchester and she could shop around for something good to buy with Mum's birthday money.

There hadn't been a present from Dad. Just a card with FOR MY DEAR DAUGHTER in silver letters on the outside. Dad knew quite well she hated yukky cards like that, and at one time if he'd sent her one he'd have written something rude inside to show he thought it was yukky too. But this one was just signed *Dad* xxx. At least he hadn't put *and Corinne*.

Patrick had sent a postcard of the picture by Edvard Munch called *The Scream*. Joanna didn't think it was a particularly cheering picture to receive on your birthday because the central figure in it looked so distressed, cowering back with ears covered. But she knew Patrick liked it because he'd had it on his bedroom wall at home, so she decided to take it as a compliment.

On the back he'd written, 'If you can't have a good

scream on your birthday, when can you?'

Her hair was almost dry. She wandered into the kitchen. Hilary was looking in the larder doubtfully.

'I hope we've got enough food. I could always do something with those gooseberries next door that are dropping off the bushes. I'm sure the old chap wouldn't mind. Just to go with the ice cream. Do you think the girls would like that?'

'There'll be heaps of food. I shouldn't bother.'

Hilary turned round. 'Darling, I do want you to have a nice time today. When you said you'd asked some friends to come over I was so pleased . . .'

'Hang on, Mum,' said Joanna. 'I can hear a car. That'll be them.'

'OK. Go down and say hello. I'll be there in a minute.'

Walking down the path to the lane, Joanna quite suddenly felt better.

They were here. They could easily have made an excuse and not turned up but they hadn't. So they must want to be here.

She was smiling, squinting into the sun as she reached the gate. The light was so dazzling that it took her a moment to realise that the two figures climbing out of the car and coming to greet her were not Leela and Becky after all.

They were Dad and Patrick.

9th February 1927

. . . rushing home to tell Father about the music room but, Alice, he wasn't pleased at all. 'I've not brought you up to take charity, Jessie,' he said. 'I'm not sure I want you up there, a girl of your class, mixing with the gentry. You shouldn't be bothering Lady Emily like this.'

I tried to explain. Lady Emily wants me up there. She does, Alice. But Father wasn't listening . . .

27th March 1927

... Lady Emily comes in most days now when I'm practising. I don't always know she's there, she comes in so quietly. Sometimes, at the end, she don't – she doesn't say anything for a while, but I just wait ...

Lady Emily sits by the window with her hands folded in her lap, listening. Outside the window the daffodils bob in the breeze and Sir Wilfred is speaking to an under-gardener trimming the edges of the North Lawn. Through the trees the sun glints on the lake.

Her mind begins to drift, passing over the little hump-backed bridge and along the Memorial Walk, seeing the acorn emblems carved at intervals along the wall, and the beloved initials R.V.M. The boom of gunfire, the terrible screaming in no-man's-land, the stench of death that have so long tortured her heart have faded, washed away by the gentle lap of water and the scent of roses. Only the three chill grottoes to pass through now before she is out into the sunlight where the fountains splash among the flowers and the steps lead up through the trees to the cross at the top where the words are carved.

'Not the same quality,' she murmurs. 'Not the same at all.'

The singing stumbles, falters.

'Beg pardon, my lady?'

Lady Emily comes back with a start to the music room.

'Your father,' she says. 'One can tell exactly where his carving ended and another hand continued.'

She sighs.

'It is true the Bible tells us we are to labour for six days and to rest on the seventh. But this was different. This was for Raymond. But Bone did what he thought was right. He had a choice and he made it. One must respect that.'

'Yes, my lady.'

'Even when we dislike the choice that has been made, we

must respect it. Without respect we are nothing. Nothing. Now, please sing again. I am sorry I interrupted. Sometimes I am . . . transported a little.'

'Yes, my lady, I know.'

'Something English this time. German is a beautiful language but . . . something English.'

Jessie collects herself and gathers her breathing into her whole body.

> Alas, my love! ye do me wrong
>   To cast me off discourteously;
> And I have lovèd you so long,
>   Delighting in your company.
> Greensleeves was all my joy
>   Greensleeves was my delight . . .

In the middle of the lake, well out of earshot of the house, Miss Pamela is boating with her friends. They've balanced a gramophone in the bows and the wail and snarl of jazz trumpets and saxophones snake across the water and go winding their way along the Memorial Walk, to lose themselves in the dimness of the woods.

Dance, laugh, they say, laugh and forget. Shorten your skirt, paint your face, drink. No more worries now; leave the old behind; the future belongs to the young. A new age has begun.

> 2nd May 1927

I told them at supper time I was going to sing for Lady Emily's friends at one of her At Home afternoons. Harold was horrible. He said, 'You'd be better off doing some work at home,' and he'd heard Mrs Kellaway was complaining up the village that I was never around when there was work to be done.

I felt bad, and wanted Father to tell Harold not to say such things, but he just got up from the table and went off to the garden.

Frank said, 'Good for you, Jess. Milk the old girl up there for everything you can while she's still around. They'll put her in the looney bin one of these days, see if they don't. Or wherever they put the gentry when they go dotty.'

Wasn't that a horrible thing to say about Lady Emily?

Nobody understands. Nobody but you, Alice. Lady Emily cares about my singing. She's going to help me become a singer. Sometimes I think Lady Emily's the only friend I got. Except for Minna . . .

'How could you, Stuart? I could just about kill you. You know that? I could *kill* you.'

Mum?

Joanna hesitated on the kitchen doorstep. That couldn't be Mum in there talking like that, the words almost spat out between clenched teeth. Mum never talked like that.

'Now wait a minute, Hilary . . .'

'No, you wait a minute. You turn up here without a word of warning, just walk in and disrupt everything . . .'

For goodness sake, thought Joanna, glancing over her shoulder at Becky and Leela who were sitting by the well, chatting. Whatever must they be thinking? Mum was supposed to be fetching the ice cream. Dad had stupidly followed her into the kitchen; now the two of them were in there having a row.

She just hadn't had a chance to explain anything to Becky and Leela. She'd still been gaping at Dad and Patrick when a second car had come bumping along the lane and she'd seen the girls waving to her. Thank goodness Mum had come running down the garden at that point, and after that there'd been nothing but a blur of people milling about.

'Um – this is my father,' she managed to say as Leela's mother drove away and they all went up the path. 'He's just sort of turned up.'

'Only for a moment,' Hilary had said, tight-lipped.

'We just called in.' He smiled at Joanna. 'To say happy birthday.'

He was wearing a yellow sports shirt that made his tanned arms and throat look gold-coloured. She'd forgotten how his eyes creased up when he smiled, his mouth half hidden by the fair beard. She turned her head away.

'Oh, right.' Becky and Leela looked slightly bemused. 'Jo, this is for you. From the two of us.'

Joanna unwrapped the parcel. It was a soft, woolly penguin wearing a red and green striped scarf.

'Oh, he's lovely. Thanks.' She thought how the penguin would cheer up her bedroom. 'I think I'll call him Percy. No, I won't, that's wrong. Um – Patagonia, that's it. Come on. I'll show you round.'

She was conscious of her father still there behind them, taking in deep breaths. 'The peace,' he was saying, 'after London. Wonderful, isn't it, Patrick?'

'Mm.'

'I had no idea you had so much land, Hilary.'

He kept exclaiming enthusiastically about everything, especially the well. Joanna had put some paving stones round it and got a few plants to grow between them. He tried to lift the cover off but he couldn't, even with Patrick's help. Joanna was pleased about that.

'Mum, they're not staying for lunch, are they?' she'd asked, agonised, while she was helping load up trays to carry out of doors. She could hear Dad's voice outside, and Becky's burst of answering laughter.

'Don't worry,' Hilary had said grimly. 'Over my dead body will they stay for lunch,' but somehow they had. Perhaps it had been too hard to make a scene in front of the girls.

They'd eaten around the well, with Hilary making

smiling conversation to Becky and Leela all the way through, while Dad tried to join in and Joanna and Patrick sat in near silence. Then Mum had got up for the ice cream.

What was Joanna supposed to do? Cope on her own? Patrick wasn't helping much, standing leaning against the plum tree. He was taller than when she'd last seen him three months ago, wearing shorts and a T-shirt with two hedgehogs on it.

She gave a sort of half-wave to Becky and Leela and took a quick look through the kitchen window. Mum had her back to her, pressed against the sink. She could just see Dad sitting at the table, rubbing his beard in the way she remembered so well.

'Disrupt?' His voice sounded as calm and interested as it always sounded. 'Oh, I don't think we're disrupting anything, are we? It all seems rather peaceful and pleasant actually. Those two friends of Jo's are nice girls, don't you think, darling, and . . .'

'Don't call me darling.'

'Sorry.'

'Don't you dare call me darling. And go away, Stuart.'

Joanna pushed her hair back from her forehead. This was dreadful. She had to get back to Becky and Leela and carry on with lunch somehow, cover everything up.

'Look, I told you. Patrick and I are camping this weekend and I thought we'd drop in with a present for Jo. You're not saying I can't bring my daughter a present on her birthday, are you? I thought we agreed . . .'

'Presents.' Hilary's voice was blistering. 'That's right, do the easy bit. Where were you when I was struggling to buy this place, struggling to make a decent home for Jo in this – this shambles of a cottage? Struggling to earn a living and do all the digging and repairs and driving on my own? Where were you then, Stuart?'

'Hang on. If you remember, you said – '

'You were nowhere. Nowhere. And then you think you can come waltzing in on her birthday with *presents*.'

Behind Joanna, Patrick said, 'Trouble?'

'Awful. Listen.'

He came nearer.

'I don't know what you're hoping to achieve, Stuart, barging in here like this . . .'

' . . . wanting to see my daughter . . .'

' . . . my daughter too, you know . . .'

' . . . won't listen to a word I say . . .'

'Oh, for God's sake . . .' Patrick said. 'This is ridiculous. Let's break it up. OK?'

'OK.'

Patrick pushed the door open. Startled, they turned round.

'Look, Mum, Dad. We're going out. All right?'

Hilary said, 'Sorry. Oh, sorry, I forgot. I'll just get the ice cream . . .'

'We'll be back,' Patrick said. 'Can I have the car keys, Dad?'

'You've only just passed your test, Patrick. And you'd have to chuck all that camping gear out. Where are you going?'

Patrick shrugged and looked at Joanna, then past her to Leela and Becky, still sitting by the well.

'The sea?' he said. 'Just the four of us. It's not far, is it?'

Joanna laughed. 'No,' she said. 'Let's do that.'

Chapter Nineteen

Jessie stands in the hall outside Lady Emily's drawing room, waiting. By her side is a carved polished chest bearing a vase of blue and purple delphiniums and a brass gong with a padded striker. A grandfather clock in the shadows behind her ticks slowly backwards and forwards.

'Jess . . .'

She turns her head and smiles.

'Oh, Jess.' Minna comes nearer, half-tiptoeing across the quiet hall, her duster in her hand. 'Don't you look nice, Jess!'

Jessie smooths her brown skirt and cream long-sleeved blouse. 'I'm glad to see you, Minna. 'Tis lonely here, waiting to go in.'

Minna looks towards the drawing-room door.

'In there? With Lady Emily's guests?'

Jessie nods. 'I'm going to sing to them. When Miss Pamela comes out to fetch me.'

Minna's eyes widen. 'Oh, Jess . . .'

'*Minna Kellaway!*' Miss Robbins, Lady Emily's maid, is on the stairs, signalling.

'Back to work at once. No hanging about by the drawing-room on Lady Emily's At Home afternoon.'

Minna throws a smile to Jessie and scuttles away.

The drawing-room door opens. Behind Miss Pamela, who wears a short low-waisted green dress with a matching bandeau tied round her forehead, Jessie glimpses a circle of ladies with teacups in their hands.

'Mummy says you're to come in now, Jessie.'

She draws a deep breath and follows Miss Pamela in . . .

'Hey, Jo, wake up. Haven't you noticed? We're here.'

'Oh . . . yes.' Joanna blinked in the brilliant light and came back to the present. Patrick was driving along Weymouth sea front looking for a parking place.

'In there . . . No, too late.' Becky leaned forward from the back seat, laughing. 'There's another one. Go on, Patrick.'

Patrick slid into the parking space, straightened up a few times and turned off the ignition with a flourish.

'Done it.'

'Patrick,' said Joanna, 'how long since you passed your test?'

'Oh, ages,' he said. 'Seems ages, anyway. Why? You're not saying I'm unsafe, are you?'

'No, no,' Leela put in soothingly before Joanna could answer. 'He's a very safe driver, Jo. And this is nice, isn't it? Come on, let's get out.'

They piled out of the car into the hot sunshine.

'Wow, look at the crowds,' said Becky.

You could scarcely see the sands, they were so thickly covered with deck chairs and sunbathing bodies. The tide was in, washing at sandcastles, dissolving them away, and shouting children splashed among the waves.

They walked along the promenade and stopped at a stall selling toffee apples and candy floss, and then sat on the edge of the promenade in a row, dangling their feet over the sands and licking.

'Sorry about that bad scene,' Joanna said. 'Back at the cottage.'

'Was it?' asked Becky.

'Oh, yes. Maybe you didn't notice but . . .'

Patrick said, 'Our fault. Dad and me, dropping in like that. It wasn't my idea, that's all I can say. I wanted to go camping in Wales. But Dad said . . .'

'I heard what Dad said,' Joanna said. 'About bringing a present. What is it?'

He scrambled to his feet. 'That reminds me. I haven't

got you anything. Let's do it now.'

They walked on towards the narrow shopping streets and started searching the little gift shops.

'This?' suggested Patrick, holding up a little plastic skeleton with black boots on.

'Or that?' Becky pointed to a pink and purple baseball cap. 'Isn't it hideous?'

'Or how about this caveman?' said Leela. 'Don't you think he's just like Sharman on a bad day?'

Joanna finally chose some earrings, a pair of tiny dangling silver and blue frogs each holding on with one hand.

'They're sweet,' said Leela. 'I love frogs.'

Outside in the street Joanna put them on, while the others sang happy birthday and passers-by turned round to smile.

They walked on as far as the harbour and watched the boats criss-crossing the water. Patrick and Becky and Leela were all talking; Joanna was happy to stroll along behind.

Later, when they were walking barefoot along the edge of the sea back to the car, Patrick dropped behind.

'How is it, Jo?' he asked. 'Living here? I mean, really?'

'OK,' she said. 'I suppose. Not like London.'

'There's this, though, isn't there?' He gestured at the sea. 'But I know what you mean.'

'What about you?'

'No problem. Quite good really. Dad has his life; I have mine. The two of us get on all right.'

Joanna stood still. 'Two? How do you mean, two of you? What about . . .?' Corinne's name stuck in her throat.

'Corinne? She's gone, hasn't she?'

'Has she? Gone where?'

'Don't know. She might be in Bali at the moment, or Bangkok. Somewhere like that. She's backpacking round the world with a couple of mates. She left weeks ago. She said she wanted a change.'

'Oh.' Joanna walked on.

'Didn't Dad tell you?' Patrick asked. 'He's always phoning you.'

'Dad doesn't tell me anything,' Joanna said. 'He just rings and says nothing much, and then he sends me some money. That's all Dad ever does.'

19th September 1927

. . . I'd peeled the potatoes and had just picked up the sewing again when Father come in. Alice, he was so angry with me.

'Sewing?' he said. 'You ought to have finished that for the day.'

I started to tell him I'd come in late, so I'd fetched the sewing in from next door to get on with while I cooked the supper, but he knew already.

Mrs Kellaway had stopped him on his way in. She'd told him I was always missing these days. That I hadn't done no – any sewing all afternoon, and Miss Mountain was going to cut my wages this week because the work weren't finished when she called for it.

'I'm finishing it now,' I said.

'Jessie,' he said. 'Where have you been all afternoon?'

I told him. Up the Big House, in the music room.

He said – oh, Alice – that I was behaving like a child, and that no good'd come of it.

'I don't want you always up at the Big House,' he said, 'as if you was one of the gentry. They don't want you bothering them. You was born at Violet Bottom, and that's where you belong. Now hurry up and get the supper.'

Later, he talked to me again, saying I should stay home more, and join in things in the village instead of

going to the Big House. He said I must trust him to know what's best for me.
I always have trusted him, Alice, ever since I were – was a little girl. But is Father always right about everything? Perhaps there's a world outside Violet Bottom he don't know anything about . . .

Joanna looked up. They were bumping in the car along the lane towards Violet Bottom.

'Grief,' Patrick exclaimed. 'Look at Dad. In this heat.'

He pulled the car up alongside Hilary's Fiat. The bonnet was up and only Stuart's rear half could be seen from under it.

'Need a hand, Dad?'

Stuart grunted and turned his head. 'Just taking a look. Your mother says there's a rattling sound developing.'

'Not surprising, coming along this lane every day.'

Patrick handed over his father's car keys, and they went round the cottage to the back garden. They found Hilary at the top of the garden, almost hidden by trees and weeds, digging up huge clumps of couch grass.

'Oh, hello, dears, you're back safely, then. Had a good time?' She wiped her hot face with her arm. 'I'll come in and get the tea organised.'

'Can't we?' Leela offered.

In the end, the three girls did the tea, while Hilary had a quick bath and Patrick took over the digging.

'Nice sexist arrangement,' Becky grinned, slicing scones and buttering them. 'Like they say in sociology lessons. Women in the house, men out of doors doing the "real" work.'

'Ah, but in this heat,' said Joanna, 'just possibly we've chosen the easy option.'

At least, she thought, it was nice to be able to choose. Not like Jessie, whose father seemed to expect her to spend so much of her life sewing or working in the kitchen.

Tea was an easy meal, with people helping themselves and sitting about in the shade to eat. At the end, Hilary produced a cake she'd managed to keep hidden from Joanna, with her name iced on it and even fifteen slightly wobbly candles.

'Blow them out, Jo . . .'

'Wish . . . Make a wish quickly . . .'

'What children you are,' Hilary observed, watching Patrick hold up Patagonia so he could make a wish too. 'You seem to get younger and younger as you grow older.'

'Only way to be, Mum,' Patrick said. 'Who wants to be out in this nasty grown-up world? Try it some time.'

'And who'd get anything done if we were all like that?'

The two of them drifted up to the top of the garden and sat on the ground, talking. The shadows began to lengthen across the grass and Stuart, having cured the Fiat's rattle, was digging steadily.

There was no doubt, Joanna admitted unwillingly to herself, as she lay in the last patch of sun with Leela and Becky, that Dad and Patrick between them had cleared a bigger area of garden in one afternoon than she and Mum had managed to do in weeks.

So, she thought, what's that supposed to prove? That men have bigger muscles? Everyone knows that already. It doesn't mean that Mum and I can't cope with living here perfectly well on our own. What's Dad up to? Either they've split up or they haven't. And again she thought: When's he going away?

When Leela's mother came to fetch the girls Hilary invited her in and soon everyone was standing about with a glass in their hands.

'It's been great, Jo,' Becky said. 'It's so lovely here.'

'Is it?'

'I wish I lived somewhere half as interesting.'

'Characterful,' said Patrick. 'Very uniquely characterful.'

'Yes, well . . .' said Joanna.

They went down to the lane to see Becky and Leela off and stood by the two cars and the heap of camping gear, waving until they were out of sight. The sound of the engine died away.

Then the four of them were alone. Hilary looked at Stuart.

He cleared his throat.

'Jo, this present. Sorry to be so late in the day. It's still in the boot of the car.'

She knew what it was even before they'd lifted it all out and carried it into the cottage, and started assembling it on the desk in her room.

She'd wanted a personal computer for a long time. There'd been no question of affording it once she and Hilary had left London.

'Oh, *Stuart*,' was all Hilary said.

'It's not new,' he said. 'Not quite. They were replacing some stuff at college and I got the chance to . . . Honestly, Hilary, it was quite cheap really. What do you think, Jo?'

'Is that the manual?' she asked neutrally, and for the next hour, all of them except Hilary pored over the instruction manual, while Joanna tried things out on the keyboard and screen.

Stuart sent Patrick down to his car for some bottles of wine, and he stood behind Joanna's chair, sipping, watching what she was doing, listening to her comments. She'd forgotten what a good listener he could sometimes be. *Could* be. He hadn't stopped to listen to her when he'd gone off with Corinne.

From time to time he waved the bottle at Hilary and said, 'Fill up, darling?' and she'd hold out her glass. She lay back on Joanna's bed, watching them; after a while, she began making occasional comments about what she did with the computers at work.

Joanna, glancing up once, saw with a small shock that it

was already completely dark outside. The moon was up, shining on the pile of camping gear still stacked in the lane.

She pushed back her chair.

'Dad,' she said. 'It's time you went now. I want to go to bed.'

'Diamonds is trumps.'

'Your deal, Jessie,' says her father.

Jessie says, 'Sorry, Father,' reaches for the cards and begins dealing round the table.

She is at a Saturday night whist drive in Lansbury Abbas Village Hall. George Bone has asked her to go with him, and wears his suit for the occasion.

The man on Jessie's left leads, followed by her father sitting opposite her. Cards are laid down, scooped up as a player takes a trick, laid down again.

'That's theirs, Jessie.'

'What? Oh . . .'

'Need to concentrate, girl. Never make a whist player if you don't watch the cards. Now your mother used to be . . .'

They stop for sandwiches and tea served from an urn. Conversation bubbles round Jessie from table to table.

'Going to have a frost tonight, you reckon, George?'

'Ah, sharp enough. Told my lad to cover up the broad beans. I like to get them well on by Christmas.'

'Getting into a useful gardener, your Leonard.'

'Not too bad.'

People speak to Jessie, but she finds nothing to say.

Walking home through the cold clear night to Violet Bottom, with her father holding her arm protectively, she thinks how dull they all were.

'You must come with me again, Jessie,' says George Bone. 'You'll soon pick it up. You're only seventeen. We'll make a whist player out of you yet.'

'Yes.' But in her mind she's already walking under the chestnut trees of Paris . . .

9th October 1927

Today, after I'd sung to her for a while, Lady Emily began talking about Paris. She told me that if Mr Raymond had lived, he would have gone to Paris to study music. There are wonderful teachers there, she said, some of the best in the world. I sang some more. Then she stopped me.

'Your future needs to be thought about, Jessie,' she said. 'What plans does your father have for you?'

I told her Father wants me to learn dressmaking, so I'll always have a trade.

She said, 'Oh, no. That would be quite unsuitable.'

I didn't say anything. After a few minutes she said, 'The chestnut trees along the banks of the River Seine are most beautiful, Jessie. Especially in the spring . . .'

23rd October 1927

. . . Lady Emily keeps talking to me about Paris. She's planning to go there next spring with Miss Pamela . . .

29th October 1927

. . . I was on my way up to the Big House today, walking past the school. The children were all out in the playground.

Mr Mahler came over to the railings to talk. He knew where I was going; he says the whole village's talking about it. And he said – oh, Alice, such nasty things.

That I shouldn't trust Lady Emily. That the gentry can never be trusted, and the way to fight them was never accept anything from them, because that gives them power over you. That . . .

I said, 'Mr Mahler, I don't want to fight them. Lady Emily's my friend.'

But at that he just burst out laughing and shook his head at me and said, 'Why are you speaking in that silly voice? What are you trying to do – copy them? Oh, Jessie, take care.' Then Miss Bradford came out ringing the bell and frowning at me, and I went off quickly up to the Big House.

Not till I was safe inside the music room and sat down at the piano, did I feel happy again . . .

It was well after midnight. Joanna lay in bed, looking at the ceiling. From below her window came a dragging sound, the chink of wine glasses, a burst of laughter. Hilary's laughter.

She and Dad and Patrick were out on the front grass, stumbling round in the moonlight, putting up the tent.

What was the matter with Mum? Had she taken leave of her senses?

Joanna turned over, hunching the bedclothes round her ears, and tried to go to sleep.

. . . I didn't tell Mr Mahler my dream. I wouldn't dare tell anybody but you, Alice. It sounds mad, I know. But I truly believe it will happen one day.

I think when Lady Emily goes to Paris next spring she'll take me with her. And she'll find me a singing teacher and she'll pay for me to have lessons. She wants me to do it instead of Mr Raymond, so the acorn won't have fallen to the ground for nothing.

There, I've told you.

Oh, I know what people would say if they knew. A girl like me. In Paris with Lady Emily.

But Lady Emily isn't like other people, Alice. She pleases herself what she does. She picked me out as special right from the start. Mr Mahler's quite wrong. I know I can trust her.

Lady Emily and me, we don't need words between

us. We understand each other. I've always known she understood me, right back to the day when . . . when you left us, Alice.

Father can't keep me back in Violet Bottom all my life. I know where my future lies.

I'll be a great singer, and you'll all be proud of me. Lady Emily, and Father and you, Alice.

Lady Emily and I understand each other so well . . .

Chapter Twenty

Joanna lifted her curtain and looked out. There was no sun this morning, just heavy grey cloud, with the view blurred by mist. Somewhere far away a cow was mooing. She looked at her watch and saw it was only half-past six.

There was no movement from the blue and orange tent on the front grass. She watched it for a minute or two, then looked at the lane and saw her father on the far side, leaning on a farm gate.

She hesitated. Then she began to dress.

He didn't hear her footsteps on the path until she was nearly there. Then he turned his head.

'Hello.'

'Hello.'

He moved sideways to make room for her. The gate was half overgrown with brambles.

'There'll be some good blackberries here in the autumn.'

'Yes.'

She glanced at him. He had less hair in the front than when she'd last seen him, and he'd combed it differently to try to disguise it.

'I thought I'd have a walk,' he said. 'Come with me?'

After a pause she said, 'OK.' When she was younger, she'd sometimes gone walking with him on Sunday mornings before the others were up.

They began walking slowly along the lane, the opposite way from the main road and the village. The surface was dry and cracked, the fringes of grass brown.

'You do have a lot of owls here, Jo, don't you?' he said after a while. 'And dogs or something, barking. They kept me awake half the night.'

'They're foxes.'

'Ah.'

The lane bent round and Violet Bottom was left behind. They passed some sort of smallholding, a couple of shabby sheds and a few cows and horses.

'Nice to have a country lane outside your front door.'

'We always go the other way. Up to the main road.'

He nodded. Then he said, 'Jo?'

She pushed her hands in her pockets. 'Yes?'

'You know that – Corinne left me? Patrick said he told you.'

She didn't answer.

'I'd have told you myself, but there wasn't a chance yesterday.'

'It doesn't make any difference, you know. Just because you and Patrick are on your own now.' Her voice was tight in her throat. 'Mum and me, we've been on our own for months.'

'Yes,' he said. 'I see.'

They passed a tumbledown cottage, its thatch stained and sagging.

'Why did you do it? You wrecked everything. Everything was fine before.' Her voice was saying it out loud at last, and it was too late to call any of it back inside again. But it was a relief, too, saying it all at last to his face.

'It was so *stupid*.' Her memory threw up a picture of Corinne, Corinne in that awful denim waistcoat, sitting hunched up on the edge of a stage where her father and his band were playing. The freckles on her white arms.

'Whatever made you go off with her? She's not much older than Patrick and me. You had Mum –'

'Jo.' He stood still. 'Darling, do you think I don't know it was stupid? That I don't wish to God it hadn't happened? But these things . . . They hit you. Like a bout of flu or something. You can't think straight. I know that's no excuse but . . . Haven't you ever wanted something as badly as that? Something, someone, that –'

'No,' said Joanna. 'I haven't.'

'Well, perhaps you will,' he said. 'One day. Then you won't be quite so ready to condemn other people.'

He walked on, not looking back to see if she was following or not.

She shouted, 'I'm on Mum's side. She won't come back to you, you know, just because you turn up here, bringing presents, getting round her, making her laugh . . .'

He turned round.

'Something wrong with laughing?' he said. 'And don't tell me what Mum'll do. That's for Mum to decide. You can't organise other people's lives like that.'

'You organised mine. We lost our house because of you. I had to leave school. I had to come down here. You completely messed my life up . . .' She couldn't go on.

'Jo, you didn't have to come down here. We gave you a choice.'

'I didn't want a choice.' She thought of George Bone, so firm and definite about what Jessie should do. '*You* should've chosen. Chosen to stay.'

He laughed shortly. 'I see. I can choose as long as I choose what you want.'

'I didn't – '

'Jo . . .' He spread his hands, his brown eyes fixed on her face. 'If I messed your life up I'm sorry. I promise I never meant to. But we can't undo it all now. We can only go on from here. So tell me what you want now.'

She stood in the lane and looked at him.

'Nothing,' she said. 'Nothing from you. You're completely hopeless, and you'll never be different. I'll never trust you again as long as I live.'

'Never?'

He smiled bleakly.

'It's no good talking, then, is it? Look, Jo. I made a mistake, I'm sorry, and I agree you've got a right to be angry.'

140

He pushed his fingers through his hair. 'But do you have to write me off completely because of it? Are you saying I'm all bad all through, and always will be, because of one mistake I made? Are you saying there can't ever be apology and – and forgiveness – and a fresh start?'

'Yes,' she said.

He turned away and started walking back. She kept her hands jammed in her pockets, and her eyes on the lane in front.

16th November 1927

...I was singing Schubert to Lady Emily, a most lovely tune and words, Alice:

> *Du bist die Ruh' der Friede mild,*
> *die Sehnsucht du, und was sie stillt . . .*

and suddenly Miss Pamela burst in through the door.

Lady Emily said, 'Sit down and listen, darling,' but Miss Pamela didn't sit down for long, she wandered round the room, picking things up, putting them down. At last she said, 'Mummy, about New Year's Eve – '

Minna's told me about New Year's Eve. Every year the family have lots of guests and a grand supper party.

'Oh surely, Pam, you'll be there?' said Lady Emily.

Miss Pamela said only if she could invite lots of her friends. She said they could put on an entertainment before supper, that it would be 'a huge lark'.

'None of that dreadful music,' said Lady Emily.

Miss Pamela said that's how all the really smart parties were these days.

'Just leave it all to us, Mummy,' she said.

After Lady Emily had gone, Miss Pamela sat on the window seat, humming. Then she said, 'By the way, Jessie . . .'

I stopped playing again.

'Come with me a moment . . .'

Jessie follows Miss Pamela to her bedroom. The pink and cream satin bed, the perfumed air, the thick towels in the adjoining bathroom all stun her into silence.

'Look at this.' Miss Pamela's holding out a dress, torn right across the shoulder.

'Mummy wants me to wear this frock for dinner this evening because some frighfully boring people are coming. And last night it – I was walking in the grounds, you see, Jessie, with a friend and it – got torn. *Could* you be an angel? Mummy won't let me have my own maid, and I hear you're absolutely marvellous at that kind of thing.'

A needle and thread is found. Jessie sits on a stool and starts sewing. Miss Pamela watches her.

'Doesn't all that music bore you, Jessie? I never knew what Raymond saw in it.'

'I'm not bored, miss.'

'Oh.' Miss Pamela examines her face in the mirror. 'I'd rather go shopping. I adore shopping. When Mummy and I are in Paris – '

'Yes, miss.' Jessie holds up the dress. The tear is invisible.

'You're an angel,' Miss Pamela declares. 'Mummy would have stopped my dress allowance for months. Now – '

She produces a huge box of chocolates.

'Help yourself. No, silly, more than that. You must have lots of people at home who'd like some . . .'

Stuart and Patrick left after breakfast.

Joanna hung around the gate while Patrick finished loading the car. Hilary and Stuart were still talking by the front door.

'Right, that's it.' Patrick slung the last bag in and

142

slammed the door. 'See you, then, Jo.'

'OK. Fine. See you.'

'I'm glad we came. It's really good here.'

Stuart came down the path. He put out a hand, withdrew it again.

'Jo. We'll keep in touch, won't we? I mean, if you want to. You know.'

She nodded without saying anything. Then she retreated to the path and stood with her mother while Stuart started the engine and began to turn the car round.

'I've never cashed all those cheques Dad keeps sending me, you know,' she said. 'I've got them all in a drawer upstairs. I'm going to tell him.'

'No.' Hilary's arm came out to stop her.

'I don't need them,' said Joanna. 'And I don't need that computer.'

'I know. But perhaps Dad needs them. Needs to give them to you. Because he doesn't know what else to say to you, Jo.'

Chapter Twenty-one

Miss Pamela and a young gentleman called Mr Ralph are dancing and singing in the music room. Mr Bobby who from his voice Jessie guesses is American, hammers out the tune on the piano:

Cuddle up, Baby, you're my honey now.
Aint it grand, dancin' to the band?
Absolutely, pos-it-ive-ly SWELL?

Jessie stands watching the dancers kicking their legs, jerking their arms. Mr Bobby seizes another piece of sheet music from the pile at his side and strikes up again:

Simply into heaven, you give me such a thrill.
Simply into heaven . . .

Mr Ralph catches Jessie's eye and smiles sheepishly. He has nice thick fair hair, she thinks . . .

2nd December 1927
. . . if only they could sing in tune. Today I couldn't bear it no – any more and I began to join in. And then – oh, Alice – Miss Pamela said I'd better take part on New Year's Eve if I fancied myself as a singer so much.

I didn't want to, truly I didn't. But the tunes are – oh, I don't know, they sort of get inside your head so you just have to sing them. And Mr Ralph wanted me to take part, Alice. He and me might even sing a duet, from *The Desert Song* . . .

12th December 1927
. . . fun, Alice. I'm still working at my 'proper' music,

of course, but it is fun.

Miss Pamela's had her hair cut very short. She said why didn't I do the same? Just imagine Father's face . . .

15th December 1927

. . . today Mr Bobby was playing a song called 'An Awful Lot My Gal Ain't Got' and pretending to be Fats Waller.

Suddenly Sir Wilfred came in, saying he could hear it right down the corridor and it was a disgusting noise.

Miss Pamela had to talk him round, telling him not to be an old-fashioned fuddy-duddy, that it'd all sound marvellous on the night when 'she'd rope a lot more people in'.

Sir Wilfred gave me a funny look as he went out . . .

17th December 1927

. . . Lady Emily says she 'fears the worst', but what can she do? She's going to have to let Pamela – Miss Pamela have her way. It gives her a headache even to think about it, she says. She talked about Paris again.

I wish Miss Pamela wouldn't mix cocktails on the piano top. Cocktails do look strange . . .

On the way out through the cold stone passage at the back of the house where the smell of cabbage lingers, Jessie passes the open door of the servants' hall.

They're sitting round the table drinking tea, the butler at one end and the cook at the other. Minna catches sight of her over the top of her mug, smiles and half gets up.

Jessie hurries out into the darkening evening . . .

19th December 1927

. . . told Father at supper.

'Do you mean, Jessie,' he said, 'you won't be

coming up to the church at midnight for the watch night service? New Year's Eve's a time for churchgoing and reflection, not theatricals. What can you be thinking of?'

Of the Big House, I nearly said. Of singing in front of all those people – and maybe even dancing, Alice! – and the lights and the applause and – oh, just of being young for once and enjoying myself. And of Paris next spring, and of singing . . . singing . . . singing . . .

On Monday morning, Joanna went back to school for the last week of term.

'Oh.' Vivien Dennis stared at her. 'Decided to come back to the bus, then, Jo-Jo?'

Joanna got up from the steps of the War Memorial where she'd been waiting for the bus.

'Yep.'

Vivien glanced round. Looking for an audience, Joanna guessed, but they were the first two at the bus stop that morning.

'I thought you liked cycling.'

'I do. But I can come on the bus if I want to. If I choose to.' She looked Vivien straight in the face. 'Can't I?'

Vivien shrugged and said nothing.

To pass the time, Joanna went round the memorial reading the names. Men lost in the First World War were listed on one side, with seventeen names including two pairs who were probably brothers or cousins; those who died in the Second World War were on the other side. There were only four of these. One of them was BONE, Leading Seaman F.

Frank?

When the bus came Vivien and several others made for the back seat.

'Look who's here. It's little Jo-Jo.'

'Fallen off your bike, Jo-Jo?'

146

'Did you get your bum numb, Jo-Jo?'

Joanna smiled at them and sat down at the front. The bus pulled away.

'Stop. Hang on. It's Richie.'

To mocking cheers and whistles, Richard Horsefield clambered up the steps. He saw Joanna and paused.

'Oooooh! Going to sit with Jo-Jo, Richie?'

'Go on, Itchy Richie. Show us what you can do.'

His face reddened, and he moved away.

'Come and sit in the back, Richie. I'll show you how to do it.'

When Joanna next looked round, Richard was half a dozen seats back, staring straight ahead as usual, his music in his ears.

Oh, well, she thought, you can't run other people's lives for them. In the end, it's their own choice.

By the last day of term on Friday, Richard was sitting next to Vivien on the back seat. When they shouted at Joanna, he didn't actually join in or look at her, but he smiled a bit at what they said, and his personal stereo was nowhere to be seen.

Christmas Eve 1927

. . . Only one more week to go. Frank and Leonard have brought in a tree from the woods, and Father was so pleased I've been careful with the housekeeping all year that he ordered a goose from the farm as a surprise. Mrs Kellaway's coming to have dinner with us.

But all I think about is New Year's Eve. That's when my true life will begin . . .

Joanna's school ended the term at lunch time on Friday. By two o'clock, she was walking along the lane to Violet Bottom.

She'd been surprised how many people she'd got to

know in her first term, how many there were to say goodbye to.

'We must get together in the holidays, Jo,' Becky had said. 'You and Leela and me. Let's meet up, shall we?'

'Oh, yes.'

Joanna had been feeling bad about the holidays. Apart from the odd day off, Hilary was going to have to keep working through the summer and the empty weeks yawned ahead with nothing particular to do.

'Let's make a definite date to meet,' Leela said. 'Saturday morning. A week from tomorrow. Where?'

'By the Hardy statue in Dorchester. At –'

'Eleven o'clock.'

'Right.'

They swapped phone numbers and promised to be there.

Joanna thought, I'll be there, certainly. But will they? Then she shook herself mentally. You have to trust people sometimes.

As she neared Violet Bottom she saw a car pulled up outside the cottages. She quickened her pace.

But it wasn't her house the visitors had come to. As soon as she unlocked the front door she could hear their voices through the wall. Two female voices, raised in order to carry clearly.

'Come on, Mr Bone, now. See what you can do.'

'Stand nice and close to the sink. *That's* the way.'

And a much older, gruffer voice.

'You think I can't manage to make a cup of tea in me own kitchen? Been doing it long enough. Leave me alone, girl, will you?'

Leonard Bone had come home.

31st December 1927

Dearest Alice,

My last letter to you in 1927. A wonderful year.

148

And next year's going to be even better.

Last night, I played some Chopin for Lady Emily, very quietly. All she wanted to do was rest, she said. And she asked me to sing the old hymns. I ended with 'There Is a Land of Pure Delight', and, as ever, I thought of you. You were the only mother I ever had, Alice.

If I succeed as a singer, it will be because of you, and because of Lady Emily. Because you both had faith in me from the start.

Lady Emily's maid, Miss Robbins, came to fetch her to dress for dinner. As she left, Lady Emily said, 'I have come to a decision about your future, Jessie. I've no time now, but tomorrow, after the performance and the supper party, we will talk about it, and I'll give you a letter for your father. It cannot be left any longer, with our Paris visit coming so soon.'

I said, 'Yes, my lady.' The letter will be asking Father's permission for me to go to Paris to study singing.

I'm ready to walk up to the Big House now. I'm not nervous. I know all the words and the music for the show tonight. I worried I might catch Leonard's cold, but I haven't. Now all I pray is I won't let the others down.

Father's in the parlour, pretending to read the newspaper. I know he's upset I'm missing the watch night service, but I'll just go in to say good night. I'll keep my coat done up, though, so he don't see my dress.

I'll write again tomorrow, Alice, and tell you everything that happened. I promise I'll write.

Your loving sister

Jessie

* * *

Joanna turned the page but it was blank. So were all the remaining pages.

Jessie had never written in the green notebook again.

Chapter Twenty-two

'Therapists, that's what they calls themselves,' said Leonard Bone.

He leaned forward and snipped some dead blooms from the rose bush that grew by his front door. 'Young maids, not scarce old enough to start school, bringing me out here to me own house, saying they'll show me how to make a pot of tea.'

He drew deeper on his cigarette.

'I told them, I been making tea in that kitchen for seventy-five years. I in't a little kiddy, needing lessons. I told them.'

'I know,' said Joanna. 'I heard you.'

'Ah. There you are, then.'

He picked up a garden fork and moved off to one of his vegetable patches. 'Got to get these potatoes lifted. Should've been done weeks ago.'

'We kept the greenhouse plants alive,' she said. 'We didn't really know what else −'

'No, you wouldn't.' He nodded and coughed. She'd heard him coughing all weekend. 'London folk like you.'

Joanna gave up.

It was the first Monday of the holidays. Mr Bone had been out working in his garden by eight o'clock. Seeing him out there, she'd thought she'd have one last try at getting him to talk about Jessie. She had to know what happened at the New Year's Eve party in 1927. And afterwards.

But it was clear Mr Bone wasn't going to talk about anything except the tests the hospital people had put him through on Friday. Hilary, who'd bumped into the frustrated therapists at the gate, had heard the whole story.

'The theory was,' she'd told Joanna, 'they'd bring him home for an hour or two to do a few tests, like tea-making and climbing stairs, to see if he could manage to live alone. Then they'd take him back to hospital and have a big discussion, and they'd decide if he could come home or if he'd have to go into care of some sort.'

She laughed. 'Mr Bone made his own decision. He just sat down in his armchair and refused to budge. Said he was home, and about time, and he wasn't going anywhere. Short of physically dragging him out to the car, they couldn't do a thing. Though I expect they'll try to get him to go back.'

They had. The doctor had arrived on Saturday morning, and they'd watched her leave again in half an hour on her own. The Rector had called on Sunday afternoon.

No doubt other people would try. But Joanna had a feeling Leonard Bone would have his way. Even when he'd been a boy, he'd never taken much notice of what other people said.

About ten o'clock she locked up the cottage and set off on her bike, without any particular idea of where she was going. It wasn't until she'd reached Lansbury Abbas and had cycled up and down the main street once or twice, that she admitted to herself that what she was really doing was looking for Miss Kellaway.

She might just happen to meet her, she thought, as she'd done once before in the village shop. And if she did, then she'd ask her what happened to Jessie Bone.

She didn't meet her. It wasn't going to be that easy.

There was some sort of conflict going on in her mind. She couldn't leave Jessie's story unfinished; she had to know what happened on that New Year's Eve. But she wasn't sure that when she knew, she'd like it very much.

'Morning, Joanna.'

152

The Rector was coming across the churchyard. 'Enjoying the holiday? You've got your neighbour back, I see.'

'Yes.'

'Wonderful old boy. What a spirit. He's going to have to accept a bit more help than he thinks, though. But I'm glad I met you, Joanna. I want to talk about the youth club.'

'I thought it closed down.'

'We're giving it another go. We've got a new leader; all we need are members. Why don't you join?'

She hesitated

'I suppose I might. I don't know how long we're staying here, though –'

'Oh, I hope you stay. We need new people in the village, especially young people. Anyway, think about the youth club.' He smiled. 'It won't just be boring old table tennis. They're hoping to do some travelling, take a minibus abroad, that sort of thing. Viv'll join, so there'll be someone you know.'

He smiled. Almost pleading, she suddenly thought, for her to say, 'Oh good'. How could she? A minibus trip abroad with Vivien would be dreadful. But perhaps the Rector really knew that, deep down, and didn't like knowing it very much.

'All right,' she said. 'I'll think about it.'

Why had she said they might not be staying? Of course they were staying. She wasn't going back to London to live with Dad or anything like that, was she?

All the way up the hill to the little circle of bungalows at the top, she was rehearsing what she'd say.

But when she finally knocked on Miss Kellaway's door, there was no need to say anything.

'Come in, dear,' called a voice. 'The door's on the latch.'

Joanna pushed it open, thinking how easy it would be for anyone to come in and steal things; though perhaps

Miss Kellaway didn't have much to steal.

She found her in the tiny back room, sitting with her feet in a bowl of water.

'Oh.' She looked up with a smile. 'I thought you was my foot lady. She's coming today. I'm just softening them up for her. Never mind, dear. Come in and sit down.'

Joanna sat on the sofa. 'Miss Kellaway – '

'I knew you'd be round some time.' The old lady's eyes were shrewd. ''Tis Jess, isn't it? You won't never leave me alone till you finds out.'

Joanna shook her head. 'I don't seem to be able to. I'm sorry, Miss Kellaway. But I will, I promise, if I just know what happened to Jessie on that New Year's Eve. You remember, when she was in the entertainment at the Big House. You must have been there . . .'

'Oh, I were there, all right. Seems like yesterday.'

She sighed. 'Pass me that towel, there's a good maid, and go and put the kettle on. We'll have a cup of tea. And then, if I must, I'll tell you. But only if you promises never to pester me about it no more . . .'

It rained that night, unseasonably; driving sheets of rain that swept across the Park and lashed the windows of Ennington Hall. Inside, the rooms were warm, full of hothouse flowers, glittering with lights and babbling with talk.

'We'd had a houseful of guests,' said Minna Kellaway, 'all over the Christmas. Oh, you wouldn't never believe the pickle they got their rooms in, some of them. Specially them London friends of Miss Pamela.'

She drew her mouth down, remembering.

'I'd only had one half-day off the whole time. I'd rushed over to see Mother at Violet Bottom for the afternoon, and found her not best pleased with Jess. Seems there'd been arguments on Christmas Day about cooking the dinner.

Mother said Jess were in a total dream all day. Anyway, on New Year's Eve . . .'

All the servants were on duty on New Year's Eve, as well as people like Minna's mother, brought in as extra help to do the washing-up. Housemaids like Minna were given clean aprons and caps, were inspected by the butler, and set to work in the supper room. Meanwhile, in the next room, a cocktail party was taking place.

'The noise! Talking . . . laughing. The butler going round with trays of drinks. The rest of us couldn't hardly hear ourselves speak.'

Minna had been carrying in a big pile of plates when one of the young ladies had spoken to her. It took her a moment or two to realise who it was.

'She had this dress on – Well, it just took me breath away. All sparkling with sequins and beads, and so short! Right up above the knee. And she had white stockings and shoes, and her face all made up with lipstick and rouge.'

And then she'd smiled and said, 'Hello, Minna,' and it was Jessie.

'She had these gloves. Oh, beautiful soft kid gloves. "Lady Emily's just given me these," she says, smoothing them like this. "I shall treasure them me whole life." And then Miss Pamela come and called her away . . .'

A sidecar. That's what Mr Bobby's talking about when Minna hurries past him with an armful of table napkins.

'You simply must try a sidecar, Jessie.' Minna thinks of Frank's dream of owning a motor cycle, and how he's promised to take her out in the sidecar one day, but this is a yellowy-orange drink.

'Oh,' Jessie exclaims, sipping it. 'So sticky. And it tastes of fruit and – and –'

'Brandy, sweetie,' says Miss Pamela. 'Isn't it too divine?'

'Mix her a Manhattan. You'll adore that, Jessie.'

Could this be Jessie, Minna thinks, talking with the gentry, *drinking* with them? Mr Ralph's smiling at her with those warm brown eyes, and then suddenly the band's playing, and they all hurry away to the improvised stage at the far end of the room and then the performance begins.

'I couldn't see much of it. Just odd moments over people's heads. But I heard it. Oh, I heard it all right. They had this band down from London. The *noise*. Three or four men, one of them a black man such as we'd never seen before in our lives, all blowing these trumpet things, and Mr Bobby at the piano, and all these young people dancing like – Well, you never seen nothing like it in your life.'

'Jessie?' asked Joanna. 'Dancing?'

Miss Kellaway shook her head. 'Perhaps. I couldn't pick her out from the rest. There was a dozen or more of them, you see, all friends of Miss Pamela, and Jess looked exactly like them. Bright Young Things, they used to call them up in London. They sang, they danced, and the audience sat at little tables drinking and smoking cigars and talking, and clapping a bit.

'But then Jessie stepped forward, and Mr Ralph, and they began to sing a duet. Something about a blue heaven. And suddenly you could hear a pin drop. And then Jess sang by herself.'

She paused.

'I don't think I'd ever heard Jess sing like it. So – so clean and sweet and lovely. After all the racketing about the rest of them had been doing. I tell you, when she'd finished, nobody didn't move in that whole room for a minute or two.'

'And then they clapped?'

'They clapped, and cheered and stamped their feet. And Jess stood there on that stage alone, and she were the queen just for that minute or two. The queen.'

156

Joanna was silent.

Then she said softly, 'And then?'

'Oh, they threw streamers, and burst balloons, and put on silly hats. But we was too busy to see none of that. Because that was when we had to be ready. Ready with the supper . . .'

Chapter Twenty-three

Lady Emily leads the way into the supper room, escorted by one of her guests. Miss Pamela follows, on the arm of Mr Bobby, and others come behind, with Sir Wilfred and his partner bringing up the rear.

Minna Kellaway, wedged behind one of the serving tables, sees them all approaching like a drift of chattering birds; the men as magpies, perhaps, in their evening clothes, the women's dresses brilliant as kingfishers.

'Champagne, Colonel?' says Lady Emily. 'And do try this lobster soufflé. It is one of Cook's specialities.'

Minna holds a plate for a parlourmaid to serve the soufflé. The Colonel turns to Miss Pamela.

'Excellent show, m'dear. Thoroughly enjoyed it. Splendid voice that last girl had. Friend of yours?'

Miss Pamela gives a little laugh, shaking her head. She calls over her shoulder, 'Bobby, don't stray like that. Come and be introduced to the Colonel like a good boy. And you, Ralph.'

Lady Emily takes a portion of asparagus and Minna hands her a silver fork. As she does so, she sees Lady Emily go still.

Minna looks past her and sees that Jessie has just come through the door.

She is smiling to herself, seemingly unaware that she is alone in a room full of couples. She comes in confidently, trustingly, and moves towards the supper table.

Minna's heart gives a twist of anxiety.

Lady Emily says, 'Pamela, dear –'

Sir Wilfred sees Jessie and comes across the room.

'Pam,' he says, 'it's too bad of you. One has a duty to

look after these people. To make sure they know where to go.'

'Sorry, Daddy, I've been so –'

Sir Wilfred lifts his hand and the butler is by his side. Sir Wilfred speaks to him in an undertone.

'Very good, sir.'

But Jessie is already coming towards them. Still smiling. She doesn't notice Minna at all.

'Oh, Miss Pamela,' she says. 'Wasn't it wonderful? When Ralph and me sang –'

'*Mr* Ralph,' says Sir Wilfred.

Jessie, dazed, turns to him. 'Beg pardon?'

'This way, miss.' The butler touches her arm. 'I'll show you where you can get your supper.'

She turns from one face to another. Mr Ralph avoids her eyes. Mr Bobby is looking amused.

'Run along, Jessie dear,' Lady Emily says gently. 'They'll find you something to eat in the servants' hall. And then you may come to my sitting room and we'll have our little talk.'

Jessie stands motionless. Her face is very pale.

'Go along, young woman,' says Sir Wilfred sharply.

Jessie's eyes are fixed on Lady Emily. 'Tell me now,' she whispers. 'About Paris, my lady. Tell me you're going to take me to Paris . . .'

Miss Kellaway smoothed out the handkerchief she'd been twisting in her hands.

'They come past the supper table and went out of the door behind me and I seen them going up the stairs, Lady Emily in her long skirt, and Jess following behind in her short one with her white stockings. And I just went on helping to serve that supper till Jess come down again. Ran down, I should say.'

'Ran?'

'Jess come running down those stairs like a – a –' Miss

159

Kellaway shook her head. 'It were almost too quick to see. Just these footsteps racing down the stairs, and a gasping, crying sort of noise, and then running across the hall, and SLAM out of the front door. The front door! Nobody but the gentry ever used the front door. And the next second I seen Jess run past the window. She'd gone out in the pouring rain.'

'What did you do?'

'I didn't stop to think. I just ducked under the table and ran out the room. The butler shouted after me, and I bumped into Lady Emily just coming in. But I kept running . . .'

Even then, Minna doesn't quite dare use the front door. She goes out through a tradesmen's entrance and runs round the side of the house to the front drive.

'Jess!' The rain's beating down and her voice is lost in the darkness. 'Jess . . .'

It's the white stockings that she sees, the awkward, uneven running.

'Jess!'

She catches up with her halfway along the drive. 'Oh, Jess, what's the matter?'

Jessie turns and stares at her. Her hair is plastered to her head and she is breathing hard.

'Come indoors, Jess. You got no coat, and you can't run in them shoes.'

'I can. I'm going home.'

'But why? Is it Lady Emily? What did she say to you?'

Jessie doesn't answer.

'Tell me. Come on, Jess.' Minna holds her arm tightly. 'You can tell me.'

Jessie's head is bent so Minna can only just catch the words.

'Lady Emily, she – she's going to Paris. With Miss Pamela. In the spring.'

160

'Yes, we all knows that, Jess.'

'She wants me to go with them.'

'To Paris? With them?'

Jessie goes on in the same flat, heavy voice as if Minna hadn't spoken.

'She said it were an honour for me, being so young. She said I'll be very good for Miss Pamela; that I'd help her to calm down, and to be a young lady. I sew so beautifully, she said. I'm just the person she wants. So long as I'm willing to learn from Miss Robbins, and do what I'm told and Father gives his – gives his permission –' Her voice breaks on a sob.

'She wants me to be Miss Pamela's maid, Minna. A lady's maid to Miss Pamela. A *servant*.'

Minna, who's been a servant since she was fourteen, flinches.

'I know now why she give me these gloves.' Jessie is tugging at the kid gloves, wrenching at the stiff buttons. 'Because she didn't want my hands to be seen. She thought they was too red and ugly for people to look at.'

'No, no, Jess.'

'She did.' She drags them off and throws them on the wet ground. 'I don't want them. I'm not a servant you can give presents to when you feels like it. D'you hear, Minna? I'll never be a servant. I'll die first.'

Minna tries to take her arm but Jessie throws her off.

'Alice knew. She knew I had to be a singer. She wouldn't never have let me be a servant. Alice knew –'

'But lady's maid,' says Minna. 'That's right at the top. You go everywhere with the family. You'd like it, Jess, once you got used to it.'

Jessie looks at her.

'I'm a singer,' she says. 'A singer.'

She turns her back on Minna and starts to walk away.

'I'm going home,' she shouts over her shoulder. 'Home to Father. I in't never coming near this place again . . .' She breaks into a run. 'I want Father . . .'

That's all Minna hears before Jessie is swallowed in the dark.

She stands there alone in the teeming rain . . .

Miss Kellaway's voice died away and there was silence in her little back room.

'You see, dear, being lady's maid *were* wonderful to me. But saying so to Jess . . . It just slipped out before I thought. And then it were too late.'

Her eyes filled with tears.

'All these years, I've wished I could call them words back again. Because they was the last words I ever spoke to Jess. I never seen her again after that night. But I can't never call them back and make everything all right again. It's too late.'

Chapter Twenty-four

Joanna took her hand off the handlebars and bit into her slice of pizza again. She was too hungry to wait till she reached home, though it was difficult to eat and avoid the potholes in the lane at the same time. Still, at least she'd been able to buy something to eat from the village shop, and she and Mum could have a proper meal tonight.

She'd stayed with Miss Kellaway for a long time, until the chiropodist had arrived and she'd seen the old lady smiling and chatting to the woman as if nothing had happened to upset her. But she had been upset; very upset.

'Look, I'm sorry, Miss Kellaway,' Joanna had said, looking anxiously at the old lady's distressed face, 'but what did you mean – you never saw Jessie again? What happened to her?'

'I can't tell you that.' Miss Kellaway shook her head. 'Don't ask me to, dear. 'Tis ancient history, and I'm too old to go back over it now.'

'But you know, don't you, what happened to Jessie that night?'

'Maybe I do. But I can't tell you. 'Tis a private matter. I've not got the right to tell you.'

'Well, who has?'

'There's only one person.' The old lady looked down at her lap. 'Only one left alive now who remembers, what with Harold and poor Frank long since passed on.'

'Leonard, you mean? Mr Bone, next door to us? He'd never tell me, Miss Kellaway.'

'I thought you said he'd told you all sorts of things already?'

'Yes, well –'

'Shown you photos and letters of Jessie's.'

Joanna shuffled uncomfortably. 'I don't think Mr Bone likes talking about Jessie very much,' she said.

'Well, then,' said Miss Kellaway, 'you'll have to do without knowing. The Bones never paraded their business in front of other people.'

She heaved herself to her feet. 'Leonard's got a right to keep everything to himself if he wants to,' she said. 'And to take it all to the grave with him if he likes.'

She looked up at Joanna with her bird-bright eyes.

'And if that's what he chooses to do, then you'll just have to accept that, dear. Won't you?'

Joanna wheeled her bike in at her front gate, munching the last of her pizza. There was no sign of Mr Bone, and she thought he must have given up gardening for the day, but when she carried her mug of coffee out of the back of the cottage a few minutes later, she could hear him talking to himself on the other side of the fence.

'Come on, boy,' she heard. 'Got to get on with it.'

'Got to get on with it,' came a higher pitched voice. 'Got to get on with it.'

Joanna put down her coffee and leaned over the fence. 'Hey, that's clever, Mr Bone. Billy never said a word all the time he was with us.'

'Didn't know the right way to talk to him, I don't suppose,' said the old man. 'He talks all right when he feels like it.'

'Got to get on with it,' said Billy, hopping about. His cage was hanging in the sun outside Mr Bone's back door.

'Little beggar don't let me have much rest,' Mr Bone said. 'Keeps me up to the mark. I got to go and see to them raspberries now. They'll be all grown up through the nets by this time, no doubt.' He wiped his face.

'Mr Bone,' said Joanna. 'Would you like some coffee? Or tea?'

He looked at her. 'I'm all right,' he said. 'I can get meself some when I wants it.'

'I know. But I've just made some and the kettle's still hot.'

His face didn't change. 'I'll have tea. Nice and strong, mind.'

Making the tea, she saw from the kitchen window to her surprise that he'd come round into her garden and was standing eyeing the back of the cottage. She went out on to the doorstep.

'Warmish day for working.' He wiped his hands down his trousers.

'Yes.' He looked much paler than before he'd gone into hospital, and his clothes seemed too big for him. 'It'll take time to get used to it again, I expect.'

'Don't do you no good, lying about in hospital all day. Mind you –' He took from Joanna the two folding chairs she was struggling to carry out to the garden – 'they was very good in there. Didn't half put me through it.'

There was a hint of what might have been a chuckle in his voice. 'Some of them young nurses and that. Turn you inside out if they could. Where d'you want these chairs?'

Joanna picked up the tray. 'Oh, by the well,' she said. 'That's where we always sit when we're in the garden.'

It was cool and quiet indoors. Joanna perched on the edge of the sofa and looked anxiously at Mr Bone.

'Are you sure you wouldn't like me to ring the doctor for you?' she asked.

He shook his head. 'Be all right in a minute.' He reached out for his tea and she saw his hand was shaking. But there was a bit more colour in his face now. Out in the garden she'd thought for a moment that he might faint.

'It's the heat,' he said. 'I in't been used to it just lately.'

She nodded.

It wasn't the heat. He'd been all right only a moment

before. It was the well. As soon as she'd suggested having tea by the well he'd swayed and dropped one of the chairs and if she hadn't put the tray down and run to support him he'd have collapsed. It was the well.

She watched him sipping tea. His hands wrapped round the mug were covered with the brown blotches of old age.

It was now or never. He has a choice, she reminded herself. He can choose.

'Mr Bone,' she said. 'There's something about the well, isn't there? Something that makes you feel very bad. Do you want to tell me about it?' Her heart was thumping. 'You don't have to if you don't want to. I just thought you might want to – you know, tell somebody.'

She waited. Through the open window she could hear Billy chirping to himself next door. Mr Bone was sitting with his white head bent, his hands still cradling the mug. He isn't going to tell me, she thought.

She said softly, 'About the well. And Jessie. I really mind what happened to Jessie, you know, on that New Year's Eve. I really mind.'

He cleared his throat with an awkward, gargling sound. She saw he was trying to put down the mug and she reached out and took it from him. He was fumbling in his pocket for cigarettes.

'Jess . . . On New Year's Eve . . .'

She took the cigarette pack from him, took one out and gave it to him. He held it between his fingers.

'She come home that night all soaking wet from the rain . . . Father and Harold, they'd just got in from church. But I had a cold. I were upstairs in bed . . . And I heard her . . . Our Jess . . .'

Stop, she wanted to say. Don't tell me any more.

But he hadn't stopped. He was telling her . . .

They rang the church bells at Lansbury Abbas to welcome in the new year, 1928. Down in Violet Bottom Leonard

Bone caught fragments of the sound gusting in on the wind and the rain as he lay in bed.

One of the bellringers was Frank; he wouldn't be home for a long time yet because ringing bells was thirsty work and they'd be sure to have a crate of beer put away somewhere. So when he did finally come home, cheerful and just a bit unsteady on his feet, he'd be certain to wake Leonard up with his usual fuss about having to share a bed with him, especially tonight when Leonard had a cold.

Leonard sniffed and felt around for a handkerchief. He hoped his cold would be better tomorrow because he wanted to get on with repairing the hen house at the top of the garden. On the other hand, if it lasted a few days more he might be able to stay off school for a bit. Only a few more months now till he could leave.

There. That was Father and Harold coming in now from the watch night service up at the church. He could hear the murmur of their voices as they moved around downstairs making tea.

One thing you could say about Harold: he never was any disturbance. Once he climbed into his narrow bed in the corner you never heard another sound out of him all night.

That just left Jess unaccounted for. Heaven only knew when she'd be back from this do at the Big House she'd got herself mixed up in . . .

'I were half asleep when the noise started. She must've run along the lane and in the front door, but the first I knew of it were the shouting, all the upset. To start with I couldn't think what it were. But then I heard Father. And Harold. And I heard Jess . . . Shouting about Paris. About being a singer. Shouting . . . I in't never heard nothing like it. She were beside herself . . .'

Leonard stands at the top of the stairs, his bare feet freezing on the lino. The voices rise to him.

167

'Go up there and tell her, Father . . . Lady Emily. She'll respect you . . . She said we got to have respect . . .'

'That frock . . .' Harold's voice. 'Make-up plastered on . . .'

'Father . . . please.'

'Of course you must take the job, Jessie. It's a great opportunity . . .'

'. . . got to study in Paris . . . Help me, Father.'

'. . . tomorrow morning. We'll go to the Big House . . . Grateful . . . Of course you will take it, Jessie.'

'. . . never . . . never . . .'

'Or you leave this house . . . can't settle down to sewing properly . . . I will have obedience in my own house . . .'

'. . . ashamed to have you as a sister . . . Remember your class . . . Aping the gentry . . .'

'. . . forget all this singing nonsense . . . Tell Lady Emily tomorrow . . .'

'No!' A shriek from Jess. 'I got to be a singer. For Alice. So's I can tell Alice –'

And a sudden silence.

'What? What did you say?'

'Alice. Alice wants me to be a singer. She –'

'Never let me hear you talk like that again. Never.'

'I got to tell Alice.' Leonard hears the back door wrench open and the roar of the rain beating down. 'I got to get to Alice . . . To the Land . . . across the narrow sea . . . Alice'll make everything all right . . .'

And the door slams.

'I heard her footsteps running down the garden path, clacking along in them shoes. I ran to the window and looked out. And I seen her in that shiny frock running through the little gate I'd made in the fence, towards the well next door . . .'

The well.

Joanna's mind froze.

They'd sat round the well laughing, having tea. She'd wanted to turn it into a quaint little wishing well. She'd wanted to drop a stone down and hear it splash at the bottom.

You'd fall and fall until you hit the icy water. And the sky would be a tiny circle far above you. And the sides smooth and steep.

She was seventeen. And she'd wanted to die. Die like that.

They hadn't let her, of course. Leonard had cried out, seeing her balanced on the edge, and Harold and George Bone had run out and dragged her indoors, fighting and soaked to the skin. Leonard remembered the water streaming off her hair and the black mascara running in streaks down her face.

They wrapped her in blankets and lectured her, while Leonard, backed in a corner and forgotten, watched. Shivering, eyes staring at nothing, she spoke only once.

'I'll do it again,' she said. 'I must get to Alice.'

Harold slapped her face, just as Frank came in, flushed and smiling above his thick scarf.

'What? . . . What's going on? Leave her alone.'

Amid the torrent of explanation, Jessie sits and shakes and stares. Frank holds her hand. Reluctantly, Harold goes out on his bicycle to fetch the doctor. Leonard, suddenly noticed, is despatched to bed.

In the morning, he's forbidden to come downstairs. Not until Dr Tripp has called again, and another doctor with him this time, and the Rector and a policeman.

When they have all left, he's allowed to come down. And Jessie has gone.

Chapter Twenty-five

'A *policeman?*' said Joanna. 'What for?'

It seemed the wrong question. But what was the right question? There were too many of them. And anyway Leonard Bone didn't answer it.

'We fastened down the well,' he said, his head still bent, the unlit cigarette limp between his fingers. 'The next day. Me and Harold. Bolted it down so you couldn't never get the cover off. And if we had a drought any summer after that, we all had to manage the best we could.'

'Didn't Mrs Kellaway mind?' Joanna asked. 'It was her well.'

'She didn't mind. She knew why we was doing it. She kept her nose out of the whole business. Everybody did. Except young Minna brought some gloves round a day or two later, real posh gloves, saying they belonged to Jess. She'd dropped them in the rain that night and Minna had cleaned them up. We put them away with the rest of Jess's stuff. We packed it all up and put it in the attic. Father didn't want it all lying around, her clothes and the photos of her and –'

'Mr Bone,' Joanna interrupted. 'I don't understand. Where had Jessie gone?'

The old man stirred uneasily.

'Father couldn't bring himself to chuck it all away, see, even then. So it stayed up in the attic year in, year out. And that's where it'd still be if you hadn't come round that Sunday, asking all them questions about Jess, stirring everything up after all this time. That night after you'd been round, I thought to meself I'd get rid of Jess's stuff once and for all. Weren't no point holding on to it no longer . . .'

'Mr Bone.' Joanna leaned forward. '*Where had Jessie gone?* Please tell me.'

He lifted his head and looked at her, then looked away again.

'Up the asylum, of course,' he said. 'The looney asylum with all the mental cases. The policeman took her away that morning.'

He saw Joanna's face.

'Didn't have no choice, did he? Father? After what she'd tried to do? And, of course, we never saw her again after that.'

'*What?*' Joanna's mouth fell open. 'You never . . . ?'

He shook his head. 'Never even mentioned her again. Not in our whole lives.'

He got to his feet.

'That's God's own truth. Now I'm going back to see to me garden.'

She caught up with him by his front door. He'd stopped to light a fresh cigarette.

'Wait, Mr Bone. Please. Don't just walk off like that, after everything you've been telling me about Jessie. I've got a right to know the rest of it.'

'What right's that, then?' He eyed her above the wavering match flame. 'You in't lived here five minutes. What's Jess to you?'

She shook her head, unable to think of an answer.

What *was* Jess to her? A girl who'd lived her life so long ago? I can't just leave her like that, she thought. On her own in some ghastly institution.

'You knows the trouble with you, don't you?' the old man was saying. 'You carry on just like her. Like Jess. She used to get herself all worked up in a state like you do, couldn't let nothing rest –'

'I told you. I care about Jessie. I want to know what happened to her.'

He sat down heavily on the wooden bench by his door.
'And I told you,' he said. 'Nothing. They put her away in the asylum. The police and the magistrates . . .'
'But why? She hadn't done anything wrong.'
He laughed shortly. 'Only tried to take her own life. That's nothing, is it?'
'It's not a crime, for goodness sake.'
'It were in them days. If they hadn't thought she'd gone looney, they could've put her in prison for what she'd done.'
She looked at him in amazement. 'You're joking.'
'Ask anybody. T'was a kind of murder, weren't it? Murdering yourself. The church were dead against it. Your life weren't your own to take like that. *Thou shalt not kill*, it said in the Bible, and that included killing yourself. That's how it were in our young day. See?'
'No.' She stared uncomprehendingly. 'Nowadays –'
'Nowadays.' He sniffed. 'You does all sorts nowadays.'
There was a silence.
'You wouldn't understand,' he said. 'The shame, if you had it in your family. It were like some disease you was afraid of catching. You had to try and hide it. We didn't never talk about it.'
'But you went to visit her in the asylum. You did, didn't you?'
He was examining his earthy fingernails.
'Father forbade it,' he said. 'None of us was to go. He said she'd put herself outside the family by what she'd done and t'would be best to cut her right out.'
'And you let him say that?' Joanna cried. 'You were fourteen, weren't you? Fifteen? The same age as me. You could've decided for yourself, couldn't you? Told your father to get lost.'
He said wearily, 'You don't know how things used to be. You didn't question nothing then. If your father said something, that's what you done.' He was staring out at

172

the rolling fields. 'All the better for it, too. You young ones get too much choice today.'

She sighed. They were going round in circles.

'So you didn't go and see her. And I bet Harold didn't either.'

'Harold married that Muriel Parsons soon after and they moved right away. But Frank —'

'Ah.'

'Maybe Frank went. If he did, he never said. T'would have been just like him, doing it behind Father's back. And he were always Jess's favourite, I knows that.'

He drew on his cigarette and coughed. 'Got an idea that schoolteacher chap — What were his name, Mahler? — he might've gone once or twice. I know he come round in a rage to see Father, but Father sent him packing. Then Mahler fell out with the School Board over something and left the village and we didn't see him no more. So then there were only Frank. And the Rector, maybe . . . Minna wanted to go but her mother wouldn't let her.'

'There was Lady Emily,' Joanna said. 'Lady Emily would have gone to see Jessie, surely. Even if she couldn't stop them putting her in an asylum, she'd have visited her, wouldn't she?'

'Lady Emily,' said the old man. He nodded to himself. 'She come round to see Father too. Just a few weeks after they put Jess inside . . .'

Lady Emily climbs out of the motor car. 'Wait here,' she says to the chauffeur, drawing her furs around her against the cutting February wind. She opens the gate of Number One, Violet Bottom, and sees George Bone and his youngest son at the side of the cottage, sawing wood into logs.

She begins to walk up the path. Dimly, a memory comes to her mind of another time when she walked up this path, carrying a basket of blackberries. The child had been so full of pain that day, pain that one sensed. Shared.

'Pain,' says Lady Emily out loud. 'It is all pain.'

For a moment she is filled with darkness again, as she had been in the war days and after, when only music could soothe her, could bring her peace. The girl's voice, and her bright face every day, had brought her much comfort.

But it had been wrong to encourage her, because it gave the child the wrong ideas. One had always to set an example, to make clear – kindly of course – where the barriers were between the gentry and the villagers. If one didn't, who knew what would happen? She blamed herself for that, for allowing the girl to get the wrong ideas.

Lady Emily sighs, remembering the music room, empty again now. It is all so sad.

'So sad,' she says.

'Yes, my lady,' says George Bone. He touches his cap to her. ''Tis a very sad business all round.' The boy goes on stacking the logs methodically. 'Will you come in and sit down, my lady?'

She sees that his face is thinner, his hair greyer. The Bones have always been one of the real old families, good solid workers, understanding the way things should be, the way they must always be. She can trust Bone to make the right decisions for the girl's own good.

'No.' She shakes her head. 'I'll not stay. I only came to say –'

To say what? She puts out a hand to him, but he moves aside from her touch.

'I had no choice, my lady.'

'Of course.'

It is all so sad. An echo comes to her mind, an echo of the girl singing at the piano:

> Alas, my love, ye do me wrong
> To cast me off discourteously;

174

And I have lovèd you so long,
Delighting in your company . . .

but she won't listen to it. And she won't think any more
about asylums, about being shut up in madhouses. She
shudders. She must never go near such places, not even
think of them. Such thoughts are not good for her.
Instead, she'll think of Raymond as a little boy, sitting
up so straight at the piano, and of the chestnut trees along
the Seine where, soon, she'll be walking in the spring
sunshine. She'll think only of happy things, and then the
darkness can never touch her.

Joanna and the old man sat in silence.

They put Jessie in a mental hospital, Joanna thought, or
whatever they called them in those days. They let her be
carried off, and they never saw her or spoke about her
again. And for what? Because George Bone decided it was
the right thing to do.

'Things settled down,' said Mr Bone. 'Father had his
work, labouring, and then a bit of proper building. Frank
went in the navy. I left school, went as a gardener to the
Big House –'

'What?' She stared at him. 'After what they'd done to
Jessie?'

He turned puzzled eyes on her. 'They hadn't done
nothing to Jess. She'd just got all these big ideas. The
gentry's all right if you keeps your distance. They taught
me the right way to do things, then let me get on with the
job. I stayed there all me life till I retired, barring the war
years. Anyhow, t'was Lady Emily offered me the job in the
first place.'

'Guilt,' said Joanna.

He sniffed, not answering.

'But, Mr Bone, Jessie must have come out of the asylum in the end.'

'Oh, she come out all right. They told me that when I went up there.'

Joanna sat up straighter. 'I thought you said you'd never visited her.'

'I didn't. This were later, much later. In the war, the second war. When I were home on leave one time . . .'

Private Leonard Bone is stationed in Yorkshire, guarding ammunition dumps. Coming home on leave involves a long, tiring journey by train, often standing in the darkened corridors, wedged with his kitbag against a solid wall of bodies.

But he comes down to Dorset whenever he can. Since his brother Frank was drowned when his ship was torpedoed, his father has looked ten years older, shrivelled up sometimes with cold as he works alone in the garden or sits in the parlour listening to the war news on the wireless.

Waiting outside the station for a bus to take him the last bit of the journey to Lansbury Abbas, Private Bone buys a newspaper, wondering what the local news is. Nearly every item is about the war in some way. A name catches his eye: the name of the mental hospital where his sister had been taken fourteen years earlier.

The next day, without telling his father where he's going, he catches a bus to the hospital, walks up the long drive and into the huge grey building.

'Yes?'

'Saw in the paper you was closing down. Sending all the patients to other hospitals to make room for war wounded.'

'That's right.'

Private Bone takes out his cigarettes, then puts them away again.

'My sister's here. I want to know where you're sending

her.' He's been unsettled by the newspaper report. Jessie's been in this place, under twenty miles away, for half his life. He can hardly remember a time when she hasn't been there.

'We'll have already informed you of that.'

If they have, his father hasn't said anything. Over the years, his father's occasionally received official-looking envelopes from somewhere, but Private Bone has never seen him open them.

'Patient's name?'

'Jessie Bone.'

The clerk goes away, comes back.

'We've no patient of that name.'

'Look again. She come here in 1928. January.'

The clerk bends over a filing cabinet. At last she straightens up, a card in her hand.

'Jessie Bone. Lansbury Abbas. Admitted January 1928,' she reads. 'Discharged June 1931.'

He stares at her. This is 1942.

'When? What date?'

'1931,' the woman repeats. '24th June, 1931. Eleven years ago.' Her voice is accusing.

24th June was Jessie's birthday. He reckons up. In 1931 it would have been her twenty-first birthday.

She'd left here eleven years ago on her twenty-first birthday.

Seeing his shock, the clerk finally comes up with a few more details. Jessie had applied to be discharged. After due consideration they'd let her go, seeing she was now an adult and was no longer considered a danger to herself or anyone else.

Presumably she'd been unwilling to return home, or perhaps his father had been asked to have her back and had refused. Anyway, on the card there's an address for her, lodgings in Dorchester, and a note to say the patient would be 'following an occupation in dressmaking'.

177

But when Private Bone asks for the address, the clerk shows to him.

Scrawled across it in red ink, someone has written:

Gone away. October 1931. Whereabouts unknown . . .

'The war ended and I come back to Violet Bottom. Me and Father settled down again.

'We hardly ever heard from Harold; just at Christmas maybe. Him and Muriel didn't have no kiddies.

'Father kept busy, right to the end. I used to drive him up to the whist drives till he were in his eighties and they stopped having them. He were still churchwarden till the last year or two when he couldn't walk so well. Even taught himself a bit of cooking; he'd have a meal ready for me when I come in from work. We got on all right, just the two of us.

'I never told him what I'd found out about Jess leaving the asylum in 1931. And I never asked him if he'd known it all along. We never talked about nothing like that.

'He were only ill for a day or two before he went, though he were well over ninety. I took some time off, looked after him. He went very peaceful. And ever since that, I been here on me own. And this is where I'm stopping.'

Joanna said, 'So your father never mentioned Jessie, Mr Bone? Not for the rest of his life?'

The old man shuffled his feet.

'Might have done. Just once. Near the end. T'was a beautiful spring morning, and the birds was all singing out in the garden. And he looked up at me as he were lying there in his big old bed. And he said something about his little maid, wanting to see his little maid again.'

He shook his head. 'Could've been Alice he meant. Or Mother, even. But I always had an idea it were Jess. Because that's what he used to call Jess in the old days, when we was kiddies. His little maid.'

His mouth tightened and he turned to Joanna.

'Now, don't you go getting ideas in your head, girl. I tell you, Father were peaceful at the end. He didn't regret nothing. I were there, and I saw.

'He knew he were right, see. He never had no doubts about that. Never.'

Chapter Twenty-six

'Help, I must go,' said Joanna, looking at her watch. 'Mum's going to think I've been kidnapped or something.'

'Let me just buy this.' Leela handed a cassette tape to the girl behind the counter. 'Then I'm going home.'

It was Saturday morning. The three girls had spent a happy couple of hours wandering round the Dorchester shops in the hot sun, looking at clothes and books and music, talking all the time. Joanna had completely forgotten she was supposed to be meeting Hilary for lunch.

'OK,' she said. 'See you, then.'

'I'll ring when I get back from holiday,' promised Becky. 'And think about the school skiing trip, Jo. It'd be fun if all three of us went. 'Bye.'

Joanna hurried towards the High Street, picking her way through the crowds of shoppers and pondering the skiing holiday. She could get a Saturday job to help pay for it.

Her mother was waiting for her on the corner.

'Sorry. Forgot.'

'What's fifteen minutes?' Hilary raised her eyebrows. 'Come on. Let's find somewhere to eat.'

Across the street, Joanna glimpsed the estate agent's where she'd first heard the name Violet Bottom. It seemed a very long time since she'd sat there looking out of the window at the sleet falling, and tried to imagine a garden full of violets.

'What about lunch here?' She stopped outside the black and white half-timbered Judge Jeffreys' Restaurant.

'Sounds a bit grim,' said Hilary. 'You know what Judge Jeffreys did, don't you? Came down to Dorset to try all those people who'd supported the Duke of Monmouth's rebellion in 1680 something, and sentenced dozens of them to death. The Bloody Assizes, it was called. Old women, children, he had no mercy on anyone. Apart from which –' she peered through the window – 'it looks full to the doors.'

Instead, they went to the restaurant called The Horse with the Red Umbrella, and squeezed their way through to the last table in the corner.

'Mum –' Joanna said, fiddling with her coffee spoon. 'You know that letter you had this morning? From Dad?'

Hilary had been examining a pair of sandals she'd just bought. She looked up guardedly.

'Yes?'

'I wondered –' Oh, come on, she thought. Don't be like old Leonard Bone who never dared ask his father about Jessie. Anything's better than that. Mum can always tell me to get lost.

'I wondered what was in it.' Since they'd come to Dorset Dad had never written to Mum as far as she knew; only to her. 'Don't tell me if you don't want to.'

'I don't mind. I didn't want you worried with it, that's all. Dad wants me to go up to London and have a chat.'

'Yes,' Joanna said, staring at the table. 'I thought it might be that.'

'Or he'll come down here again if it's easier. He wants to talk about the situation. About the divorce. He wants –'

'He wants to come crawling back to you,' Joanna interrupted angrily.

'Don't, Jo.' Hilary shook her head. 'Don't put it like that. All Dad's suggesting is, we might try getting together again. Perhaps. If I want to.'

'He's just looking for someone to take care of him now Corinne's skipped off. We're all right as we are, Mum. We've got on well, haven't we?'

Joanna's chest felt tight. I gave everything up for Mum,

181

she thought. I was on her side. I wanted to support her. Now it's being thrown back in my face.

'I don't know how you can even think of it,' she said.

Hilary leaned across and touched her hand. 'Darling, you've worked so hard. And you've never moaned about any of it. But now I think –'

'What?'

'Oh . . .' Hilary's hands dithered in the air. 'I don't know. We've been married a long time. And . . . perhaps money shouldn't matter, but it does. It'd be much cheaper for Dad and me to keep only one place going instead of two. And then . . . Dad keeps saying he's so dreadfully sorry. He says he wants to make a fresh start.'

'He would do, wouldn't he?'

Hilary was staring out of the window. 'I never wanted to break up in the first place. It was – Oh, anyway, I'm not really sure I can ever settle here. I mean, sometimes I think it's all right but –'

'I can,' Joanna retorted. 'I'm used to it now. I'm not going to uproot myself again.'

'It hasn't got as far as uprooting yet. There's my job for one thing. I wouldn't want to lose that. I might never get another.'

'Well, there you are, then.'

Hilary sighed. 'Oh, Jo, what a muddle. What shall I do?'

'I don't know,' said Joanna. 'Don't ask me.'

She sat, head down. I can't run their lives for them, she thought. Since when did parents ask their children what they ought to do?

I bet Dad *is* only trying to come back because Corinne's left him. He'll do it again one day. Anyone with any sense would never trust him again. Never.

Never say never.

Because that's what George Bone said.

I'll never have you in this house again.

I'll never go to the asylum and see you.

182

I'll never so much as speak your name again.
And he forced everybody to fit in with his ideas of what was right and what was wrong.

Whereas Dad . . .

Dad's awful in some ways. Sometimes I think he hasn't got a clue about what's right and what's wrong. Look at the way he's been carrying on. Just doing exactly what he wanted without even noticing he was hurting other people. He's just like Sharman at school, and Vivien and the rest, all of them doing exactly what they feel like, trampling over other people, people like me.

But there's one thing Dad can do that Jessie's father couldn't.

Dad can say he's made a mistake.

Jessie's father was a good man, a loving man, and he probably did his best to bring up his children the way he thought was right.

But he couldn't cope with Jessie, and he trampled all over her; and then he couldn't say he might have made a mistake and he was sorry.

But Dad could. Perhaps Dad's hopeless in some ways, but he said sorry to me that morning we walked along the lane. And I went off home without speaking to him.

Forgiving people is a terrible risk. But you've got to give it a go sometimes.

She raised her head and looked at her mother.

'I can't tell you what to do, Mum,' she said. She stood up.

'But I expect there are things . . . You could leave it for a while, couldn't you, and we could all try meeting a bit more often and see what happens. I mean, we aren't living in Thomas Hardy's day. There are cars and trains, aren't there, and phones and things? We could just see how it goes, couldn't we?'

Never say never.

*   *   *

It was dark when they reached the cottage and the owls were calling. Joanna and Hilary had spent the afternoon swimming and sunbathing in one of the little bays, and then walking along the cliff tops in the evening sunshine.

As they bumped along in the car round the last bend in the lane, Joanna saw Mr Bone's bedroom light go on.

I know, she thought. I know what I'm going to do in the morning.

She heard him moving round in the next-door bedroom, and then his footsteps going stiffly downstairs. She rolled over and looked blearily at her bedside clock.

'Ten past six?' she said to Patagonia. 'On a Sunday morning?'

That must be what a stay in hospital does for you.

She lay and read for a while. Then she dressed and made some tea, took a cup upstairs to Hilary, and went outside and round to next door.

'Hello, Mr Bone.' She found him in his back garden, balanced on a pair of steps, cutting the hedge with a pair of shears. He'd already done half of it.

He nodded to her.

'You're busy.'

'Got all out of shape. Shouldn't have been allowed to grow like that.'

'No.' She managed not to apologise. It was his hedge, after all, and he'd chosen to come back here to live. Anyway, he seemed to be making a pretty good job of it.

'Mr Bone. Mum and I wondered if you'd like to have Sunday lunch with us today. If you've got time.'

He turned round, rubbing his chin with the back of his hand.

'Could have, I s'pose,' he said. 'Could have time. Round about one o'clock, something like that?'

'Yes, fine.'

'I'll have to come away soon after, mind,' he said.

'There's a bit of football on the telly I want to watch this afternoon.'

'Oh, right.'

He went back to cutting the hedge. After a minute he said, 'You can thank your ma for the invitation. Save me getting me own dinner, that will. Give me a bit longer to get this garden back in order.'

Walking round to the front of the cottage, Joanna could still hear the steady clip-clip of the shears.

As she'd hoped, his front door opened when pushed. People were much less afraid of burglars here than they'd been in London.

She went quietly inside and into the living room and stood studying the photographs on the sideboard.

George and his wife, arm in arm and stiffly upright. Frank, smiling in his sailor's uniform: December 1939. Leonard, pushing his father's wheelchair along a seaside promenade.

And the children in their little oval frames: Alice, Harold, Frank and Leonard. And the empty oval.

Joanna looked up at Alice on the wall.

'They were afraid,' she said to Alice. 'That's what it was.'

Afraid of Jessie because she was different from them. Afraid of all the music and the passion that poured out of her. Afraid that the Big House people and the Violet Bottom people would get all mixed up so you wouldn't know where you belonged any more. Afraid of anything new and unknown.

She was like a bird fluttering in a cage, wanting to get out. But they crushed her because they were afraid. Until she found her own way out and was lost to sight.

The green notebook had been put away in Joanna's bedroom. It's safe with me, she said to Alice. Quite safe.

185

Jessie wanted to tell someone and she told you. Or me. I'm not sure I know the difference any more.

There was no way now, so long after, of knowing what the end of Jessie's life had been. But it didn't matter. She could let Jessie go now, back to the past.

She went out again into the little front hall. There was only room for one piece of furniture here, an old wooden chest half hidden by the coats that hung on pegs above it. There was a small gap between the bottom of the chest and the floor.

Joanna bent down and slipped the little oval photograph into the gap. It could so easily have fallen there when the old man was carrying Jessie's belongings out to the lane for the dustmen to take away.

His cottage might be shabby, but she'd noticed each time she'd been in it that it was remarkably clean. She guessed Leonard Bone took as much care with his dusting and polishing as he took with his garden. And even if he didn't find the photograph, they'd surely be sending him a Home Help one day, and she would find it.

The photograph had been separated from the rest for so long that a little more time wouldn't matter at all. Just so long as he eventually put it back where it belonged.

If he wanted to. He had a choice. She mustn't forget that. Only if he wanted to.

Chapter Twenty-seven

Gregory Nolan set down the pile of plates and watched his father and uncles cooking at the barbecue, their faces sweating in the January evening sun. In a couple of days' time he'd be stepping off the plane at Heathrow. He wondered what the weather would be like in London. It could even be snowing. That'd be something new to see.

'Hey, Greg, got all your packing done, have you?' asked one of his friends.

'Not much to do. I'm just taking my backpack and stuff like that.'

'Hopeless.' His mother lifted her eyebrows. 'You'd think he was going for a weekend instead of three years. So casual.'

'I'll be all right.' He grinned at her. 'I'll be studying too hard to get into mischief, won't I?'

'Now, don't nag the poor lad, Alice,' his father called from the barbecue. 'Remember he'll be thousands of miles away by Friday.'

Gregory wandered round the garden, chatting to his friends and family who had come to his farewell party. It was good of his parents to organise it, he thought, but he wouldn't be sorry to be on that plane tomorrow, on his way once and for all to England.

'Hello, Gran.' He sat down next to her on the seat under the eucalyptus tree. 'I'll get you something else to eat, shall I? Can't have you and Grandad sitting there with empty plates.'

She smiled at him, nineteen years old and her youngest grandson. 'We're quite all right, Greg. There's no need to wait on us. But it's very nice food. A beautiful supper . . .'

There'd been another beautiful supper once. But she

hadn't been allowed even to come near it. It wasn't for people like her.

'Ladies and gentlemen . . .' Her son David was on his feet, proposing a toast to Greg. She made a rueful face at her husband and took a sip of wine. Neither of them could get used to the idea of having a middle-aged son; two of them, in fact. Even Alice, their youngest child, had a few grey hairs.

The trouble was that, inside, she felt no older now than she'd felt that day she'd sat on the doorstep at Violet Bottom with Minna.

'. . . coming back in three years' time with all the glittering prizes of the music world at his feet . . .'

Gregory saw her slip her arm through Grandad's and knew what she was thinking. Three years was a very long time at Grandad's age. Of course, he was wonderful. After a lifetime of teaching, he was still organising meetings, writing to the newspapers and radio, still so alive and active. But nevertheless . . .

Three years, his grandfather thought. What's three years? Only the same time that Jessie was in that place before I managed to get her out. And what were those three years, measured against all the good years we've had together since?

For a moment, the old smell of the asylum came back to his mind: floor polish and disinfectant and plain human misery and hopelessness. Every Sunday afternoon he used to walk up that long drive; used to sit with her, trying with all his energy to make her smile, to make her see that she wasn't mad, that there was some hope ahead of her.

Later, once he'd badgered the authorities into agreeing that she could go as soon as she was twenty-one, there had been the visits to her lodgings in Dorchester; their plans. That had been better, even though by then he'd had no job. They'd walked through the meadows by the river, and ridden on a bus along Weymouth sea front, and he'd seen her relax, beginning to look forward to things again.

By the time they'd travelled up to his family in Manchester to get married and to arrange their passage to Australia, she was looking quite like the old Jessie again; like the young girl he'd started to fall in love with that day she'd stood on the other side of the school railings and tilted her chin and said to him, 'Mr Mahler, I don't want to fight them. Lady Emily's my friend . . .'

'Tom, dear.' She touched his arm. 'I'm just going to talk to Greg for a minute.'

She and her grandson strolled across the lawn to the small swimming pool behind the hedge. Gregory found her a chair and then sat on the springboard, dangling his feet in the water.

'You must try to get to Paris for a day or two at least.' She smiled to herself. 'I believe it's beautiful. The chestnut trees along the river . . .'

'Sure, if there's time. I'm going to have to work very hard at the piano, you know, if I'm going to make it.'

'I know, darling. But you'll do it all right. If that's what you want, you'll do it.'

Not an acorn falls into the ground but it may become an oak tree. If it was too late for me to become quite the singer I'd hoped, I think I still gave a lot of joy to people when I sang. I've got a room full of cups and certificates and mementoes at home. And I've done my best to pass on what I've learnt to younger people. It's all been all right. All of it.

'Greg?'

'Yes, Gran?'

'Just one more thing . . .'

At one time, there'd been letters from Frank. She and Tom had managed to give him an address before they left England, and now and again letters would arrive, or post-cards from the ports his ship called at, always with a cheery message, and a hope that one day they'd meet.

She'd write back. And always she included a message for Father.

There was never a message back from George Bone. And in 1941 Frank's letters had stopped coming. A bit later there'd been a note from one of his shipmates, telling her that he'd been lost at sea, saying that he'd always promised Frank he'd contact her if anything happened to him.

Since then, she'd concentrated on her own young family, on building up a happy life with Tom.

But there was still hope.

'When you're in England,' she said. 'You might find you've got time to go down to Lansbury Abbas in Dorset one day. To Violet Bottom.'

She saw the parlour again, with Alice's photograph smiling down on them, and Father looking at her with pride as she read the figures to him from the housekeeping book.

'Go and look at the house where we were all born. Where your great-grandfather lived. He was a fine man, Greg. And just ask anybody you meet. Ask if there's anybody who remembers Jessie Bone.'

She smiled. Leonard wouldn't be really old. Not yet. Nor would Minna. Neither of them would ever have moved far away. There was such a lot to hope for.

'Tell them,' she said. 'If you find anybody, Greg. Tell them I'm here.'

Author's Note

Some of the events in TELL ALICE may seem to today's readers difficult to believe. Yet some of the more melodramatic happenings are in fact completely authentic.

For example, *The Story of Piddlehinton: a Dorset Village History* records that a man called Frank Woodland was dismissed from his employment by Lady Debenham because he refused to work on a Sunday. He had eight children, and eventually had to take a job as farm labourer. His daughter Emily went into service at the age of fourteen, earning £12 a year as a 'between maid'.

Committing suicide by jumping down wells sounds most unlikely, yet a lady now aged eighty-nine described to me how several people had done this during her childhood in a Buckinghamshire village. Modern means of suicide such as a drugs overdose or carbon monoxide poisoning were of course not available.

The 'putting away' in the asylum undoubtedly went on; often it only came to light when the institutions were closed in the 1970s and 80s. My informant told me of the shame and the feelings of embarrassment that families in villages often went through after a suicide attempt; suicide was, after all, a crime until 1961.

Girls were often pushed into the 'little mother' role that befell Jessie, when their mother or older sister died; this was well described in the CTV series *Out of the Doll's House*.

The name Violet Bottom follows Dorset tradition: I found Bramble Bottom, Little Puddle Bottom, Well Bottom and even Kiddies Bottom all on the map near Dorchester when researching this book.